MATTHEW'S CHILDREN

BY
CJ CARMICHAEL

MILLS & BOON

First published in Great Britain 2009
Harlequin Mills & Boon Limited,
Eton House, 18-24 Paradise Road, Richmond, Surrey TW9 1SR

© Carla Daum 2008

ISBN: 978 0 263 87654 3

23-1109

Harlequin Mills & Boon policy is to use papers that are natural, renewable and recyclable products and made from wood grown in sustainable forests. The logging and manufacturing processes conform to the legal environmental regulations of the country of origin.

Printed and bound in Spain
by Litografia Rosés S.A., Barcelona

Hard to imagine a more glamorous life than being an accountant, isn't it? Still, **CJ Carmichael** gave up the thrills of income tax forms and double entry bookkeeping when she sold her first book in 1998. She has now written more than twenty-five novels and strongly suggests you look elsewhere for financial planning advice.

This book is for my youngest daughter, Tessa,
who is leaving home to start university this year.

I could not love you more, or be more proud.

Thanks To:

My writing friend and lawyer Elizabeth Aspinall,
Constable Chris Terry
and criminal lawyer Simon Lord
for taking the time to talk to me about
their areas of expertise.

CHAPTER ONE

IF JANE PRENTICE HAD SEEN Matthew Gray in the elevator, she would have taken the stairs. But as she stepped on board, she was reading case notes and didn't spot him until the doors were gliding shut behind her.

"Hi, Jane."

That voice. It still had the power to remind her she was a woman first. Lawyer second. She stuffed her papers into a side compartment of her briefcase, then looked at him. And away.

"Matt."

An awkward pause followed. At least they weren't alone. Two men in business suits flanked her, neither man familiar. When the elevator stopped at the twenty-eighth floor, only she and Matt stepped off.

"Going to the partners meeting?" Matt asked, as they headed in the same direction.

She nodded. *Crap. Obviously, so was he.* What was going on? Over the past year they'd become adept at avoiding each other. She'd requested an office on the opposite side of the building from his. By tacit agreement they'd begun attending alternate partners meetings. And she and Matt both avoided places they used to go together, like Sully's Tavern and the deli downstairs.

Everyone at Brandstrom and Norton was in on it; even the managing partners no longer assigned them to the same cases.

A year ago the rumor had been everywhere. *Matthew's marriage is in trouble. And Jane's the other woman...*

"Russell dropped by my office this morning," Matthew explained. "He made it pretty clear my presence was mandatory today."

"I wonder why."

"Some new case he wants me to work on."

Jane sneaked a sideways glance at him. The year had taken its toll, adding some lines and a few gray hairs, but he was still handsome in that intellectual, Robert Downey, Jr, way of his.

"I was sorry to hear about you and Gillian."

"Were you?"

She hadn't expected him to challenge her, and wasn't sure how to respond. A part of her *was* sorry, naturally. Matthew didn't deserve what had happened. He was a good man, honorable in the old-fashioned sense of the word.

Yes, he'd spent too much time at work. Yes, he'd neglected his adolescent son and much younger daughter.

He wasn't perfect.

But who was?

They rounded a corner, and the open door to the conference room was now in sight. Matt's voice became coolly professional. "By the way, congratulations on the Laskin case."

She could feel her cheeks grow hot. They may have avoided each other the past year, but he'd kept tabs on her. "I was lucky with the judge."

"You're too modest. The story in the *Hartford Courant* was pretty complimentary."

The admiration in his voice was contained, yet unmistakable. She tried to meet his gaze again without losing her composure. But she couldn't.

So she made her way into the room, where she headed for a vacant seat next to another of the junior partners at the firm. "Hi, Susan. How was your weekend?"

While Susan chatted about her three kids and husband, Jane organized her papers and located a pen.

"…and then Jeremy tells me it's his turn to bring the morning snack for circle time! I had to leave Jack to handle breakfast and drive to the market to buy enough fresh fruit for twenty-five children. And when I get in the car, what happens? Jack's run me low on gas again!"

Jane murmured a sympathetic comment, feeling anything but sorry for Susan's predicament. Did her colleague have any idea how lucky she was? She and Jack had been married ten years and had three healthy children.

Finally, Jane found her pen amid the clutter at the bottom of her briefcase. She inhaled deeply and checked around the table. All the familiar faces calmed her. *This* was her family, and now that her father had moved to Texas, it was the only family in Hartford she had.

She'd been working at Brandstrom and Norton since she'd graduated from law school twelve years ago. Eve Brandstrom had hired her, and had become her mentor and close advisor.

Eve made a powerful ally. Some claimed she was too hard, too driven. But Jane had never found her so. Now she caught Eve's eye and smiled.

I hope I look that good when I'm in my fifties.

Eve returned her smile, but her eyebrows were knit. When her eyes shifted in Matthew's direction, her frown deepened.

Had Eve noticed them walk in together? That she might be keeping an eye on the two of them was more than a little discomfiting.

Eve, along with two junior lawyers from the firm, had been present at the restaurant last January when Jane and Matt had met for their disastrous, final lunch together. Eve's party had been sitting at a different table, but in plain view.

All three of them had seen everything. The whole sordid scenario.

Jane wanted to believe that one of the other lawyers—and not Eve—had subsequently spread the rumors about her and Matt. But she couldn't be sure. She and Eve had never talked about that day. Jane had hoped that eventually it might be forgotten.

The expression on Eve's face told her it hadn't.

ALL THE USUAL SUSPECTS were in place as Matthew entered the conference room. Sensing Jane would prefer it, he headed to the other end of the table from her, putting as much distance between them as possible. Unfortunately, when he sat down he realized he'd selected a seat with a perfect view of her. If he wasn't careful, he'd end up staring at her throughout the meeting.

In an attempt to distract himself, he glanced around. The conference room was in the southwest corner of the twenty-eighth floor. Two walls were all windows; the other two were covered with paintings by New England artists. The room was impressive. The inlaid wood table was itself a work of art.

But he'd seen this room a hundred times before.

Whereas Jane he hadn't seen in a year.

And now that he had, one thing was clear. She still hit him like a shot of caffeine—jolting him, making him feel more alive. How could she not? Besides being one of the most intelligent lawyers in the firm, she was also kind, compassionate, honest and decent.

Her attractiveness and beauty were all the more potent to him because of these other qualities. And it was precisely because of them—in particular the honesty—that he'd worked so hard to stay away from her.

That hadn't been easy.

But to do otherwise wouldn't have been fair to her. Rumors had buzzed around the office after the "lunch from hell"—as he tended to think of it. When he'd announced his divorce from Gillian, the gossip had started again. One of his coworkers had screwed up the courage to ask him, "Is this about Jane?"

"No," he'd insisted, but his protestation hadn't had much impact on the opinions at the office.

He'd wanted to protect Jane, but he hadn't known how. The best he could do, it seemed, was keep his distance.

No doubt about it. This past year had been hell. For most of it he'd lived in an apartment full of rented furniture that he hated. He'd never felt more alone. His mother was busy with her new life in the seniors' complex she'd moved to, and his two brothers were preoccupied with lives of their own.

His ex-wife considered him a cheating liar. And while his three-year-old daughter still loved him unconditionally, his adolescent son didn't want anything to do with him.

On top of all that, he had lost his valued friendship with Jane.

"Coffee, Matthew?" Davis Norton was the oldest senior partner and the only surviving founder of the firm. He was approaching seventy and rarely took cases. Still, he never missed a partners meeting.

"Thank you."

Davis filled a bone china cup with steady hands and passed it to Matthew, then returned the carafe to the sideboard and settled in his place at one end of the table.

Sitting at the other end of the rectangular table was Russell Fielding and, next to him, Eve Brandstrom.

Russell was one of those men who had finally grown into his looks in his fifties. With his steel-gray hair, strong jaw and broad shoulders, he had the sort of distinguished presence that juries loved.

Eve, also, had developed an air of distinction as she'd aged. Thick, dark hair framed a face grown more attractive with the sculpting hand of age. As she peered over stylish, turquoise glasses, her eyes were clear and sharp, as was her mind.

Although the firm bore her family's name, Eve's preeminent position here had little to do with nepotism. She'd never married and seemed to live for her job, having few outside interests. Since her father had passed away two years ago, she was determined to do his memory proud.

In addition to the three senior partners, there were six junior partners at Brandstrom and Norton, including Jane and Matthew. All were in attendance today. Each had nodded at him earlier, but not one would meet his eyes now.

Something was up.

Matthew felt a surge of adrenaline. Just what was this case Russell wanted him to handle?

He checked his BlackBerry. One minute before nine. Russell, who usually chaired these things, was a stickler about starting *exactly* on time.

Matthew's gaze slid over to Jane. He just couldn't stop himself. He noticed details he'd been too flustered to pay attention to in the elevator. She was wearing a black suit, impeccably tailored, and a slim-fitting shirt. The thin red stripes in her white shirt brought out the color in her lips and on her cheeks.

She wasn't looking at him. Wasn't looking at anyone in particular, really. She nodded when Davis offered her coffee, and when he'd finished pouring, she brought the cup to her lips with a steady hand.

Matthew gave her credit. She had to know everyone in the room had watched them walk in together. The curiosity in the air was almost palpable, yet she affected the utmost nonchalance.

As she set the cup back on the saucer, Matthew's attention moved to the long, fine bones of her fingers. Her gold watch dangled on her elegant wrist. As if she could feel the spot where his gaze lingered, she pushed the watch higher on her forearm.

She looked around the room, let her gaze rest on his briefly, then carried on. Jane was one of few who had resisted the lure of the BlackBerry, and she set a pad of paper on the table and clicked her pen to release the nib. She was ready.

Russell cleared his throat. "Good morning, colleagues. I trust you all had a pleasant weekend. Before we discuss new business, we'll go around the table with our usual updates."

Though he hadn't expected to be at this meeting, Matthew was prepared when it was his turn to speak. Most of his cases were minor, not worthy of discussion in this forum. But he'd be going to preliminary hearings on a manslaughter case next week. He summarized the facts, answered a few questions, then leaned back in his chair as the spotlight shifted to the coworker on his right.

Again Jane's gaze sought him out. This time several seconds passed before she glanced away.

His heart was drumming so loudly he almost didn't hear Russell as he proceeded to the next order of business—assigning new cases.

Two phrases leaped out at him, though.

"...sexual misconduct involving a minor...soccer coach...."

Matthew's mind stopped wandering as he noticed everyone was looking at him again. Was this the case?

"I realize no one in the firm will be clamoring to handle this one."

Russell had that right. Sexual misconduct involving a minor. You couldn't get much uglier than that. Usually, such cases were assigned on a rotating basis. Who had handled the last one? Matthew knew it hadn't been him.

"According to the schedule, this one is Jane's."

Matthew, like everyone else in the room, turned to her. Jane's face paled, but she showed no other reaction.

"However, in this instance," Russell continued, "our client has requested a specific lawyer. Matthew Gray."

Matthew felt sucker punched. "Who is this guy? Did he give any reason for requesting me?"

"He's the coach of your son's soccer team. He says you met at the season start-up party for the Blazers."

Matthew did his best to organize his thoughts. "You must be talking about Wally Keller."

"That's correct."

"What, exactly, is Coach Keller alleged to have done?" *Please let it have nothing to do with Derrick.*

"The police are investigating him for sexual misconduct with the twin sister of one of the boys on the team."

Matthew only knew of one guy on the team who had a twin sister. Right now, he couldn't remember either of their names. "Do you have a name?"

"Sarah Boutin."

His memory quickly provided him with an image of the girl. An outgoing blonde, tall and thin like her brother. Matthew recalled the boy's name now; it was Robert. The Boutins lived in the same neighborhood as his ex-wife and kids. He had a dim recollection of Robert and Sarah coming over to play with Derrick when they were younger.

"Is she okay?"

"She's at home with her mother, so physically she must be fine. But she has claimed sexual abuse, and medical examination has confirmed this. We don't yet know the details of what transpired."

Details. Matthew's stomach turned. "And she said Coach Keller was responsible?"

"That's right."

He swore. "I don't want anything to do with this case."

"None of us does, Matt. But the client is asking for you. He told me you seemed like a decent guy and he wanted your help with this."

Damn it. Why had Keller done that? Matthew

would have been pleased to refer him to several excellent attorneys.

With all eyes on him, Matthew shook his head. "Isn't it obvious I can't do it? I have a conflict of interest. My son is on his soccer team."

"That makes it a gray area, I agree. Which is why I've decided to put two lawyers on this one. You'll be on the team primarily to hold Keller's hand, walk him through this. You know how tough these cases can be."

Hold his hand? Walk him through it? "I'm a pretty expensive babysitter."

Everyone chuckled, including Russell, but the senior partner didn't back down. "I have no doubt you'll provide the client with good value. Besides, this is an excellent career opportunity for you. This case has the potential to be high-profile."

"What if I'm not that ambitious?"

Again there was laughter. No one in the room considered it possible that he wasn't joking.

Actually, one person didn't laugh. Jane's gaze met his, warm with sympathy, but also a hint of apprehension. Matthew thought he understood why.

As if he could read Matthew's mind, Russell nodded. "You'll be working with Jane on this one, Matt. That's who I've decided should be lead lawyer."

"But—" He and Jane objected at the same time.

Russell held up his hand. "I know the two of you haven't worked together in a while. But we're a small team here and that can't go on forever. Eve and Davis agree with me."

He said nothing more, and neither did Jane nor Matthew. But as soon as the meeting was over, Matthew intended to have a strongly worded chat with Russell. From the grim expression on Jane's face, so did she.

CHAPTER TWO

"THIS IS IMPOSSIBLE, Russell." Jane sounded calm. The only sign betraying her agitation was the end-over-end rotation of her pen as she jabbed it again and again on a blank page of her notepad.

Matthew recognized the nervous habit from years of observing Jane in court. It was something she fell back on when she felt cornered.

The three of them were alone in the conference room now. The other partners had scattered at the official closing of the meeting. Jane and Matthew had moved to sit on either side of Russell.

"She's right," he said, hoping his composure was a match for hers. "We can't work together."

"Aren't you being dramatic? A year has passed, guys. The divorce is behind you, Matt. We can't do anything about that now."

Russell made it sound so cut-and-dried. From a legal standpoint, Matthew supposed he was correct. But emotional wounds couldn't be healed with a court document. A year had passed but they were all still hurting.

"Come on, Russell. You've made Jane the lead lawyer. She might as well handle the case on her own. I'll just get in her way."

"Wally Keller is scared, Matt. Can you imagine how it feels to be accused of something like this? What do you suppose he'll tell his wife? His kids? He knows you and he trusts you. Can you blame him for wanting a familiar face on his team?"

Matthew paused, thinking about how Wally had gone out of his way to help his son at the beginning of the season. Unlike most of the other boys on the team, Derrick hadn't started his adolescent growth spurt yet and was self-conscious about his size. At the team's first practice, the coach proposed a strategy for dealing with the bigger boys on the field. His suggestions had given Derrick a whole new confidence in his abilities.

"If Matt has to be on the case, then let him handle it on his own," Jane insisted. "Or assign another lead lawyer."

"No one else has the time right now. And since your Laskin case wrapped up last week, Jane, you're the obvious choice. Besides, it *is* your turn."

She bowed her head, acknowledging the logic of his argument.

"Matt. Jane. Let's be reasonable adults here. We can't let a bunch of ugly rumors—and I have no doubt they were just rumors—destroy two excellent careers. Everyone remembers how well you two used to work together. Your skills complement each other, and I have every faith in your ability to provide Wally Keller the best defense this firm can offer."

With that, Russell rose from his chair. He slid a file to the center of the table. "This is all I have so far. Mr. Keller is scheduled for an initial consult at one o'clock tomorrow. I've taken the liberty of booking the small conference room for your meeting."

He left the room, diplomatically closing the door behind him. Matthew fixed his gaze on the folder. As he watched, Jane reached for it and pulled it across the table.

Their eyes met.

"I suppose Russ has a point," Matthew began tentatively. "In a firm this size we can't avoid each other forever."

"Really? I thought we were getting damn good at it."

He laughed. Then quickly sobered. "Not that I ever wanted to avoid you. I hate that you were stuck in the middle of my personal disaster."

"It wasn't your fault."

"There are some who would disagree."

"I can't believe Gillian actually spied on you." Jane clapped her hand to her mouth. "Sorry. I shouldn't have said that. But it's just so wrong. You're the most honest person I know."

"I appreciate that. But I'm not sure it's true."

She gave him a doubtful glance. "Who have you ever lied to?"

Acknowledging the churning feelings inside himself, Matthew knew the answer. "The most important person."

"Your wife?"

He shook his head. Despite Gillian's accusations to the contrary, he'd never deliberately told her anything but the truth. His deceptions had gone much deeper.

"Myself."

BEFORE SHE'D MET Matthew Gray, Jane had assumed that men like him didn't exist anymore. Regardless of the progress women had made in the workforce over the past few decades, she still encountered sexism on a regular basis: biased judges, condescending prosecutors, and clients who thought only a man could handle the job. Jane had seen it all.

Matthew displayed none of those prejudices. From her first day at the firm, he'd treated her with the same respect he accorded all his colleagues.

His underlying gallantry had nothing to do with male dominance, but was simply a manifestation of his good manners and consideration.

It hadn't taken long for him to become her favorite lawyer to work with at Brandstrom and Norton.

She'd always known he was married, and it had never occurred to her that that might cause any problems. Unlike some of her other married colleagues, he did not flirt with women, not even in so-called harmless ways.

Jane had felt perfectly safe putting in late hours with him, and had never expected that the real danger didn't lie with him, but with her.

She still couldn't pinpoint the moment she'd fallen in love with him. Maybe it was when she'd seen how tenderly he'd interviewed a scared young mother fighting for custody of her child. But it might just as easily have been as Jane watched him shred the testimony of a prosecutor's star witness who'd traded away the freedom of Matthew's client.

Now, as she tried to focus on the case notes in front of her, she wondered if it truly was possible for the two of them to work together again.

She cleared her throat. "So what do you know about this guy?"

Matthew seemed surprised, then amused. "That's how you want to handle this? Straight to the business at hand?"

"Do we have another choice?"

"You could tell me what's been going on in your life over the past twelve months."

Through various internal channels he would have heard about the professional stuff. "You mean my personal life?"

"Well…yeah."

Her cheeks turned hot. She was blushing. How ridiculous was that? His interest meant little. Matthew probably felt a measure of responsibility for her happiness. Not that he ought to, but he was that sort of man. Probably he wanted reassurance that her life hadn't fallen apart the way his had.

And of course it hadn't.

You needed to have a personal life in order for it to

fall apart. And she didn't. She hadn't had a serious romantic relationship in years. The last one had ended so badly it had taken her over a year to recover. And then, just when she'd been ready to start dating again, she'd realized she was falling for Matthew, a married man.

Ever since, work had been her only safe outlet.

But she couldn't tell him that.

She struggled to think of something to say. "I joined a health club last September."

He laughed. "That's your news?"

"Hey, it was a big step for me."

"Do you ever go?"

"To use the sauna and the hot tub," she confessed.

"I joined a health club, too."

"The Executive Club downstairs?"

"Yes."

"I thought I saw you there the other day." She'd gone to unwind in the sauna after a grueling day in court. As she'd headed for the change rooms, she'd noticed Matthew running laps, his face so tense she'd ached for him.

"We'll have to meet for a workout sometime."

She nodded, assuming they wouldn't. "How are your brothers?"

"Nick's still busting his butt, hoping for that promotion to detective. And Gavin's living the small-town dream in New Hampshire, with his new wife, Allison, and his daughter, Tory."

Though she'd never met anyone in Matthew's

family, Matthew talked about them a lot. She had a soft spot for Gavin, who had lost his daughter Samantha, Tory's twin, in a terrible accident about two years ago. "I heard that Gavin remarried. That's good."

"Yeah, it is. Allison's been great for him. And for Tory. Even Mom likes her."

"And how's your mom? Is she handling the changes in your life okay?"

"She's not happy about the divorce. But since she sold the house and moved into a condominium for seniors, she's doing a lot better. She's made friends and isn't so anxious anymore."

Matthew gave her a speculative look tinged with sympathy. "How's your dad? Have you visited him lately?"

"Two Christmases ago." Back in the days when she and Matt had worked together often, she'd confessed how ambivalent she felt about her dad's second marriage. She was glad he was happy, but his life was so full now he didn't have much time left for her.

Oh, boo-hoo, Jane. You're an adult. Stop feeling sorry for yourself. She straightened her back. "So. Are we all caught up now? Can we finally discuss our case?"

Matt laughed ruefully. "Back to business, huh?"

"You said you met Coach Keller at a party for your son's soccer team. So you know him quite well then."

"Not really. This is the first year he's coached Derrick's team. It's a volunteer position."

She flipped a page in the file Russell had left for them. "The notes say Wally Keller is new to Hartford."

"That's right. His family moved from Maine for the start of the school year."

"We'll have to find out why." Any hint of scandal behind the relocation wouldn't bode well.

"Yes. He told me he was transferred through the accounting company where he works, but of course we'll need to check that."

They went through a list of discussion points regarding their new client. He'd been married fifteen years, had a son Derrick's age and a younger daughter. His work history was solid, and he had no priors.

"He sounds like your average upstanding citizen," Jane concluded at the end of half an hour.

"Let's hope appearances aren't deceiving."

When they left the conference room, it was almost noon. In the old days they would have gone to the deli downstairs for a quick sandwich.

But times were different.

They stood in the hallway looking awkwardly at each other, before Jane finally broke away to catch the elevator. She thought Matt was watching her, but when she glanced back, he was gone.

He was probably planning to eat lunch in his office. That was what he seemed to do most days.

Down in the lobby she picked up a chef's salad at the deli. But as she sat at a small table for two and tried to eat, her stomach refused to cooperate. She set down the plastic fork and gave up the effort.

Her career meant everything to her, and it hung in the balance. Russell Fielding had been tactful, yet he'd made it clear that this past year had put a strain not only on her and Matt, but on their coworkers, too.

For twelve months she'd been resisting the truth, but now she faced it. If she couldn't get past this thing for Matthew, she would have to find another job.

AFTER THE MEETING with Jane, Matthew ordered a sandwich to be delivered to his desk. Work had been his sanctuary in the past, he certainly needed the escape today. He opened the top file from a stack and stared at lines of type that blurred into illegible scratching.

How did Jane feel about working with him again? Was any part of her, however small, happy at the prospect?

He was divorced now, so it wouldn't be the same as before. He wouldn't have to hide his admiration…or fight his attraction.

Yeah, right. Who was he kidding? After all he'd put her through, he was lucky she'd consented to work with him. Let alone anything more.

His phone rang. A client was in trouble. He'd been driving under the influence of alcohol when he'd had a traffic accident. His second that year.

Silently, Matthew swore at the stupidity of some people. "Here's what you need to do…" he said.

Hours later, Matthew was talking to another client, this one in an even deeper mess, when he noticed the time. Ten minutes to seven. He scrolled down on his BlackBerry, then groaned. Derrick had a soccer game tonight, at seven-thirty.

In the past, Matthew had missed a lot of Derrick's soccer games. But no longer. He'd vowed that this spring he would catch every game he possibly could.

He offered his client one last piece of advice, then scheduled a meeting for the following day. Quickly, he closed down his computer, then left the office. Derrick hated it when he came to the games dressed in his business attire, so he took the time to change at the Executive Club in the basement. That he might see Jane here crossed his mind, but he didn't.

Finally, dressed in casual jeans and a sweater, he rode the elevator to the parking garage. Once he was behind the wheel of his Audi, he punched the address of the soccer field into the GPS.

Now that his son was in the league for older kids, he was expected to play all over Hartford. Matthew wasn't familiar with most of the fields anymore, and the GPS had kept him from arriving late more than once.

As he drove past a burger joint, he realized he was starving. Hours had passed since that sandwich at noon. He longed to stop, but was afraid that if he did, he'd miss the opening kickoff. In the end, he arrived at the game five minutes early. The spring sky was cloudy, but rain didn't appear imminent. As he headed for the bleachers, he spotted Gillian amid a group of other soccer moms. He settled on a bench as far away from her as possible.

He didn't want his relationship with his ex-wife to be hostile—it wouldn't be healthy for his kids. Yet he felt powerless to change things. Every conversation he tried to have with Gillian ended in an argument, with her making the same accusations and drawing the same—erroneous—conclusions as ever.

She hadn't reacted to his arrival, yet he knew that somehow she had seen him. If ever he missed a game, she would be the first to call him on it.

His son's team, the Blazers, was wearing blue-and-yellow uniforms. He searched for lucky number six, Derrick's number, and spotted him goofing around with another kid, rough-housing on the sidelines.

Stuff like that never went on when Coach Keller was in charge, but of course Wally Keller wasn't present today, and neither was his wife, Leslie. Andy Crosby, another of the soccer dads, was attempting to fill in. Judging by the flustered expression on his face as he jogged from one boy to another, giving instructions that were largely ignored, he wasn't finding the job easy.

Coach Keller's son, Daniel, was among the boys on the field, but Robert, Sarah Boutin's brother, was absent. Matthew watched as Daniel, a large, athletic boy, took shots at the net. Matthew wondered if he'd been told what his father had been accused of. Did the other kids on the team know, too?

The referee blew his whistle and play began. The Blazers came out disorganized and weak, and five minutes into the game the opposing team scored. The team was hurting without their usual coach.

But something else was going on, Matthew realized.

One of the Blazers' midfielders went out of his way to jostle Daniel, who was playing center.

Well, that answered his question about how much the kids knew.

Poor Daniel.

By halftime the team was down two goals. The sun was low on the horizon and Matthew decided to use the short break in action to run to his car and grab his sunglasses.

To his discomfort, his ex-wife followed him.

CHAPTER THREE

"HAVE YOU HEARD about Coach Keller?" Gillian asked. Her voice was stiff and censorious, as if somehow Matthew was to blame for the situation.

He slipped on his sunglasses. "Yeah, I have. Where's Violet?"

"With a sitter." Gillian sounded impatient. "Who told you about Keller?"

He wasn't about to reveal that Wally Keller was now a client of the firm's. "Who told *you?*" he countered.

"The soccer association sent out an e-mail. I didn't see your address on the distribution list, though." Her eyes narrowed suspiciously.

"Maybe you could ask them to add it for me. I would appreciate receiving e-mails about Derrick's team."

"Fine."

He guessed she would have argued if she'd had any basis to do so. But since she claimed to want him more involved with Derrick's life, how could she?

"Have you heard how Sarah's doing?" he said. "I noticed Robert wasn't here."

"Neither of the Boutin kids was at school today, according to Derrick. I heard they were receiving counseling."

"That's good."

Gillian shook her head. "I still can't believe this could happen in our neighborhood. We need to screen our coaches more thoroughly from now on. It makes me sick to think that I trusted Wally Keller."

"Maybe Keller isn't responsible for what happened to Sarah."

Gillian rolled her eyes. "Innocent until proven guilty."

She'd heard him say the phrase so often the words had no meaning to her. Matthew couldn't blame her. Most people he met felt the same way. Maybe because not that many of them had ever been accused of a crime they hadn't committed.

"Please don't tell any of the other parents you think Sarah is lying."

"I didn't say I thought Sarah was lying, Gillian." But…it was possible.

In the course of his career, Matthew had seen it happen often enough. Children who were hurt or scared sometimes lied or made up scenarios for reasons that adults didn't always understand. While Sarah's sexual abuse seemed irrefutable, he wouldn't automatically condemn Wally of the crime.

And he certainly felt sympathy for the Keller family. Leslie and her children didn't deserve the grief that this was bringing them.

He didn't like to think that Wally deserved it, either.

AFTER THE GAME, Matt waited on the sidelines for an opportunity to speak to his son. The boys lined up to shake one another's hands, then each team huddled around their coach for a postgame wrap-up.

Due to his smaller size, Derrick was easy to pick out in the crowd. He appeared despondent after the loss, and left the field with his head low.

"Nice effort." Matthew clasped Derrick's sweaty shoulder. He referenced a play late in the second half when Derrick had set up the center for a goal. "That was a beautiful pass."

For a second his son's eyes gleamed. Then he shrugged. "We still lost."

Unfortunately, that one goal hadn't been enough.

Matt bit back the platitudes. *You can't win them all* wasn't something he wanted to hear after a bad court case. Neither was *There's always the next one* or *At least you gave it your best.*

The truth was losing sucked. "You must be tired. I noticed you were playing shorthanded."

Derrick nodded. "Some of the guys are thinking of quitting the team."

Matthew needed a second to figure out why. "Because of Coach Keller?"

Derrick nodded. "Now we have to find a new coach."

"What about the father who filled in today?"

"He doesn't know a thing about soccer. He just stepped in at the last minute so we wouldn't have to forfeit the game."

"Oh." Matt slipped his hands into the pockets of his jeans. Derrick shot him a quick look, then grabbed his soccer bag.

Silence stretched between them, and Matt realized that his son was waiting for something. Oh, cripes. Derrick wasn't hoping Matthew would volunteer for the job, was he?

"I wish I could help, but my work is too unpredictable." He was making most of the games, but no way could he handle practices, plus all the prep work in between.

"I know that." Derrick sounded angry. "I didn't ask you to, did I?" He swung his soccer bag over his shoulder and started toward Gillian's car. His mother was sitting in the driver's seat, waiting.

Matthew didn't want the evening to end this way. "How about we grab a slushy? I'll drop you off at home later."

Derrick paused. He seemed tempted. But then he shook his head. "I've got an English assignment due tomorrow. I'd better go straight home."

"Sure." Matthew swallowed, but the hurt didn't go anywhere. It stayed lodged in his throat, its favorite hangout.

He was being dissed, but he couldn't blame Derrick. How many times had his son asked him for a little time, and Matthew had put him off because of work? It was such a cliché, the workaholic father, the needy son. Yet the pattern had been set and he didn't know how to change it.

All he could do was keep trying. "Okay. Get your schoolwork done and I'll see you on the weekend."

"You mean next weekend, right? I'm at home this one."

"Actually, no. Check the calendar, son. You were with your mom last weekend, so it's my turn."

"Fine." Derrick nodded curtly, then upped his pace to a jog. Matthew watched him go, wishing he'd been able to give his son a hug. But there'd been no opportunity.

Or none that he could find.

"I CAN'T FREAKIN' BELIEVE this." Wally Keller had refused a chair, and was pacing the small meeting room. He had a broad face, stocky body and intelligent but now frightened-looking eyes.

An average dad, Matthew thought. In terrifying circumstances.

It was Tuesday afternoon, one o'clock. Jane had offered Wally Keller coffee at the beginning of their meeting, and when he'd refused, she'd poured a cup for herself. She was leaning against the sideboard now, mug in one hand, eyes trained warily on their new client.

Matthew didn't blame her for being cautious. Keller was radiating tension and anger. Innocent people tended to behave that way when they were falsely accused of a crime. Unfortunately, guilty people often reacted the same way.

"You think you're doing a good thing, coaching

your kid's soccer team. A lot of parents can't be bothered. They drop their sons at the field, then drive off to run errands or go back to work."

Matthew glanced down at his notebook. Guilty as charged. Not so much now, but in the past he'd definitely been one of the parents Wally Keller was describing.

"And this is my reward." He stopped moving and gripped the back of a chair with enough strength to drain the blood from his knuckles.

For a moment Matthew trained his eyes on those hands. They were average-size for a man, but to a kid they would seem mighty intimidating. For a moment he found himself speculating. *Was Keller guilty?*

But that wasn't a productive line of thought.

"This must be hard, Wally." He and Jane had agreed that since Keller knew him, Matthew would lead the conversation.

He wanted to begin by offering a bit of hope. "Just because the police called you in for questioning doesn't mean that charges will be laid."

"God, I hope you're right."

"But we still have to be prepared," Matthew continued. "We have a lot to cover. Why don't you sit down."

Wally hesitated, then nodded. Once he was seated, Jane took a place at the table, too. With a subtle nod in Matthew's direction, she picked up her pen, indicating that she would keep notes, leaving him free to concentrate on the questions.

She'd always been able to anticipate where he was

going in a way none of his other colleagues managed to. He smiled appreciatively then turned to Wally.

"We need to establish your relationship with Sarah Boutin."

"There was no relationship!" Wally's face reddened.

"Would you know her if you saw her?"

"Well, sure. Her twin brother plays for the Blazers. She used to watch all the games and often showed up at practices, too."

"The practices?" That was unusual. Mostly, it was just the players who attended those. "Why?"

"She said girls' soccer was boring and she liked working out with the boys better. I used to let her join in on some of the drills and exercises."

"So you treated her just like the other kids on the team?"

"Well, not always. Sometimes she would follow me around and try to talk."

"Did you have time to do that?" Jane seemed surprised.

"Not really. When you're running a practice, you're pretty busy. Setting up exercises, watching the kids, providing feedback."

"What did Sarah like to talk about?" Matthew asked.

"I didn't pay that much attention. Like I said, I couldn't. But I do recall that she talked about her dad a lot. Her folks split up not that long ago. I gather her father left town. It was pretty obvious she missed having the old man around."

Matthew nodded. At the preseason soccer party

Sarah and Robert's mother, Claudia Boutin, had cornered him. She'd told him that she, too, would soon be divorced. There had been a few awkward moments when he'd wondered if she was hitting on him.

He'd been rescued from potential embarrassment when Wally had asked for a volunteer to barbecue burgers. Matthew had practically raced out to the deck.

"It was pretty obvious the kid missed having her dad around," Wally continued. "Frankly, she was disruptive, and I was often tempted to send her home, but I felt sorry for her and I didn't."

From his expression, he clearly regretted that decision. So did Matthew.

"Were you ever alone with her?"

"I've been thinking about that, and I can only think of one time."

Damn. He'd been hoping there'd been *no* times. "What happened?"

"A thunderstorm brewed up during practice last week. I had the kids phone their parents to pick them up."

Matthew remembered that night. Gillian had been busy with Violet's gym class, so she'd phoned to see if he could get Derrick. He'd been at a meeting on the other side of the city, too far to reach the field on time. So he'd called Derrick and suggested he catch a ride with a neighbor.

"Did Sarah and Robert's mother show up to get them?"

"No. I didn't realize it, but Robert had accepted a

ride home from a teammate who lived on the same block as the Boutins. I guess he forgot about his sister. When the storm hit, she was the only kid left on the field. The lightning seemed close. It was safer for the two of us to wait in my car. But her mother never did show up, and eventually, I drove Sarah home myself."

Matthew glanced at Jane and saw the same dismay in her eyes that he was feeling. It was an emotion he did his best not to reveal as he asked, "How long were you and Sarah alone together?"

"Fifteen minutes, maybe twenty. If you count the drive home, half an hour." Wally seemed to understand the potential danger in this, because he exploded with anger again. "What was I supposed to do? There was lightning, for God's sake."

"Where was the assistant coach?" Matthew wondered.

"Gone home." Keller's voice was little more than a growl. "He'd checked off all the boys' names, so he decided he could leave."

"Didn't he realize Sarah was there?"

Keller shrugged. "You'll have to ask him that. I sure as hell did."

"Right." Matthew got up from the table. "I'm going to grab a coffee. Changed your mind, Wally?"

The man hesitated, then nodded. Matthew left the room. This would give Jane an opportunity to question Wally without appearing to interrupt him. When he returned, Walter was in the middle of an answer.

"We were settling in okay before this happened." He accepted the coffee with a faint thanks.

Good. She was filling in some of the background info. Matthew sat back in his chair and let Jane continue. She asked their client about his job and how the kids felt about the move. When she was done, Matthew had some more questions about Sarah. Over an hour passed before the meeting was finally concluded.

Together he and Jane escorted Keller to the elevator. Just before he got on, Wally turned to him.

"Thanks for helping me out, Matt. Three nights ago I met with the board of the soccer association. I could see the doubt on their faces when I told them I was resigning and why. Half of them have already decided that I'm guilty. But I'm not." He stared Matthew straight in the eyes, his expression sincere and earnest.

Then the elevator arrived and he left.

"Do you believe him?" Jane asked quietly.

"Yeah. I think I do."

Jane gave him a skeptical glance before sinking back against the paneled wall with only partly feigned exhaustion. "That was tough."

Emotionally, yes, it had been. But Matthew's adrenaline was flowing. He hadn't felt so up for a new case in a long time. He didn't kid himself why.

It was great working with Jane again.

"Want to go for a drink?"

She looked surprised, but her voice was collected. "Are you sure that's a good idea?"

"I'm not married anymore, Jane. I believe it's allowed."

CHAPTER FOUR

SULLY'S TAVERN WAS A HALF flight of stairs below street level, just off Bushnell Park, and though it was a favorite haunt of trial lawyers, Jane hadn't been there for over a year. She felt Matthew's hand at the small of her back as she descended into the familiar, dimly lit haven. Matt guided her to one of the booths and her black skirt slid smoothly over the leather seat.

The music playing in the background was too subtle for her to place. She glanced around. Fewer than half the seats around them were occupied. She tented her hands on the clean, cool tabletop and waited until Matt was seated, too.

"It's so quiet," she said.

"Yeah. It's weird to be here on a Monday."

In the past they'd frequented Sully's at the end of the work week. A bunch of them would gather here from Brandstrom and Norton—not just the partners but all the lawyers, and some admin staff, too. On Fridays the tavern was packed, the music loud and raunchy.

"It feels like a different place."

"Too quiet?" Matt half rose. "We could go somewhere else."

"This is fine." The truth was she would feel uncomfortable wherever they went, because she hadn't been in a social situation with him for a very long time.

She'd avoided Sully's this past year in order to avoid *him*. In her heart she knew the reasons for his divorce had nothing to do with her. Yet, her conscience demanded that she keep her distance while he was going through the process of ending his marriage. Just knowing how she felt about him—and that her feelings had the potential to become much deeper if she let them—had been reason enough.

A server came and they placed their orders. Jane's emotions steadied now that she had a drink in her hands. She swirled the glass and watched the ice cubes jostle in the translucent amber liquid.

Sometimes, when she was playing dangerous "what-if" games with herself, she wondered what would have happened if she and Matt had met each other much earlier—before Gillian. Jane was pretty sure he found her attractive. And she knew he liked her. So was she crazy to believe they might have ended up together?

Yes. She had only to recall the two failed relationships in her past for her answer.

"You're avoiding eye contact." Matthew sounded amused.

She lifted her head, glad he couldn't possibly be aware of what she'd been fantasizing about. She tried to keep meeting his gaze, but eventually, she had to blink. The blue of his eyes was such a piercing shade.

"You should be a judge. You would be impossible to lie to."

"Is that what you're planning to do?"

She smiled. "No. But admit it. Being alone like this. It must seem as strange to you as it does to me."

All amusement drained from his expression. "I don't want it to feel that way, Jane. I want us to be able to work together. To be friends."

She swallowed. It didn't sound like much. Yet it was. "It's difficult not to remember the last time we were…"

Matt's expression turned grim. He finished her sentence for her. "The last time we were alone in a public place together?"

"Yes."

"I'm so sorry about that, Jane. I can't tell you how sorry."

His regret was deeply sincere, and it only made her respect him more. The scene hadn't been his fault. It hadn't been either of their faults. On the afternoon of their fateful lunch together, they'd been discussing business, a case that was before the court, when Gillian Gray had found them.

Jane could still picture the surprise on Matthew's face. The gallant way he had immediately stood, reaching for a third chair so his wife could join them.

In those first seconds he hadn't noticed Gillian's fury. But Jane had. Because it had been directed at her.

"What are you doing with my husband?"

Nothing, Jane had been about to say. But before she

could utter a word, Gillian Gray had grabbed a goblet from the table and hurled the white wine it contained into Jane's face.

She would never forget the shock. The intense humiliation.

"Madam." A server had been at her elbow almost immediately, leading her to the women's washroom.

Behind her, she'd heard Matthew speaking to his wife. "Are you crazy?"

Not the right words to appease. Gillian had raged at him; she'd really let him have it. At the door to the ladies' room, Jane had paused, unable to stop listening until Gillian—finally out of foul words and insane accusations—turned on her heel and marched out of the restaurant.

From across the room Jane had met Matthew's gaze. She'd seen the abject apology in his eyes before he'd raced after his wife.

All of that would have been terrible enough. But Eve Brandstrom and two other lawyers from the firm had witnessed the entire debacle. Jane still didn't believe Eve had said anything to anyone else.

But the other lawyers hadn't been so discreet, and soon the story was circulating Brandstrom and Norton. Jane couldn't go anywhere without being confronted with the speculation and curiosity in her coworkers' eyes.

She had reacted by keeping her mouth shut and avoiding Matthew as much as possible. Since he'd done the same, it wasn't difficult.

Now she couldn't believe she was across the table from him again. She still wasn't sure this was wise. He might be an unmarried man legally, but he would never be "available" where she was concerned.

"I should have apologized at the time," Matthew said. "But I was afraid it would only feed the gossip at the office if anyone saw me talking to you."

"I understand. I imagine you had enough to handle at home." Jane had heard about Gillian's subsequent obsessive calls to the office. If she couldn't reach her husband, she would yell at the poor receptionist. A few weeks later, word got out that Matthew had spent the night sleeping in his office, on the couch.

Soon after came the announcement that Matthew and Gillian Gray had separated.

A year later, the divorce became final.

And now that the marriage was at last over, Jane had to know the answer to the one question that had puzzled her for so long. "Why did Gillian think we were having an affair?"

Surely, in this day and age, his wife had expected some of Matthew's colleagues to be female. Why assume the worst?

Was it possible that Gillian's feminine intuition had sensed Jane's attraction—an attraction Jane had worked so hard to stifle—and had reacted instinctively against it?

"By that point in our marriage, Gillian was on the lookout for things to fight about. She noticed your name on my BlackBerry a few times, heard us talking on the phone, and it raised her suspicions."

"But why?"

"Things hadn't been going well between us for years. Opposites may attract, Jane, but they shouldn't always get married. Especially not when they want different things from life."

"You and Gillian were opposites?"

"In many ways. She was a drama major when I met her, and I found that exotic at the time. But after a while her incredibly emotional nature became draining."

"I know what you mean by emotional."

"Gillian could turn almost anything into an argument. That, too, was draining. Gradually I began staying later and later at work. After Derrick was born and Gillian opted to be at home full-time our problem became worse. Without the creative release of her career Gillian grew more restless and unhappy."

"Did you consider hiring a nanny?"

"I'd just talked Gillian into that when she unexpectedly became pregnant with Violet."

An old pain surfaced, but Jane refused to focus on it. This wasn't about her. "How about you? Did you want a second child?"

"Secretly, I was thrilled, but I couldn't admit it to Gillian or she would have accused me of getting her pregnant on purpose—which wasn't the case. At any rate, when Violet was born, Gillian loved her as much as she loved Derrick, of course. She just transferred all her anger and resentment to me."

"I'm sorry."

He shrugged. "The fights got worse. I began

avoiding home even more, which only made Gillian angrier."

A sad story, especially when Jane considered the children and how confused they must have felt. Still, she was reassured to hear that the Grays' marital problems went back so far. It relieved some of her guilt. Not all. But some.

"Gillian resented my long hours at work. At the same time, she pressured me for money for home renovations and a family vacation in Europe. I guess I took the easy way out, opting to spend more hours at the office rather than deal with her moods at home. I figured once I had my promotion to partnership life would get easier."

"But it didn't."

He shook his head. "As you know, they only pile on more cases once you make partner."

"That's true. But you can set boundaries," she added gently. She'd never heard of Matthew turning down a case or refusing to work on a weekend.

"Gillian had legitimate complaints," Matthew acknowledged.

"Did you guys consider counseling?"

"I was willing. She wasn't."

Jane grimaced.

"It wouldn't be so bad if it wasn't for the kids." He skated his glass over the slick surface of the table.

He kept a photograph of his son and daughter on his desk. Jane had noticed it this morning as she'd passed by his office on her way to the supply room, which she no longer avoided.

"How are Derrick and Violet doing now?"

"Violet's fine. She's young and the new situation hasn't upset her routine very much, since she always sleeps in her own room. But Derrick's pretty angry."

"At you?"

"Yeah. He definitely views me as the culprit. He rolls his eyes every time I mention anything to do with work. I'm struggling to achieve a better balance in my life, but sometimes my efforts seem futile. Especially when my son makes it obvious he'd rather be with his mother."

"Matt…" It wasn't like him to be so negative.

"Sorry. We've been talking about this too long." He leaned over the table. "What's new with you?"

She hadn't expected the conversation to turn so quickly. "I joined a health club," she offered weakly.

"So you said. Anything else? Are you dating anyone?"

The question was thrown in as if meant very casually, but to Jane Matt's eyes burned as he waited for her response.

"Not right now." She met a lot of men in her line of work, so there were always opportunities for dating. None of the men she'd gone out with this year had held her interest, though. They all fell short compared with Matt.

The truth was there had never been a man who affected her the way Matthew did. Not even her first love, in university; or the man she'd almost married five years ago. Even now she felt like a nervous teenager on a date rather than a competent professional sharing a drink with a colleague.

"We haven't discussed the case yet," she realized.

"We aren't here to discuss the case."

"We aren't?"

"No, Jane, I hope—"

He stopped talking when his BlackBerry buzzed loudly.

"I thought I'd switched this off," he muttered as he reached for the thing.

Jane assumed that was what he was about to do now, but a glance at the number changed his mind.

"It's my son," he said, rising from his seat as he spoke. "I have to talk to him. Can you give me a minute?"

"Sure." Her lips felt stiff, but she forced a smile, averting her gaze rather than watching him walk away from the table.

She couldn't help but think back to that other time over a year ago. This interruption was far less dramatic, but it was an equally effective reminder that where Matthew Gray was concerned, she had to guard her emotions very carefully.

MATTHEW WOULD HAVE interrupted his conversation with Jane for only two people in the world. Since Violet was too young to use the phone, that left Derrick.

"Hey, son. What's up?" He strode through the pub and out the door. Lingering by the stairs, he plugged his free ear to block the traffic noise.

"I'm calling about the game on Friday."

"I'll be there."

"Don't bother."

"Pardon?"

"We still don't have a coach."

So none of the other parents had volunteered. As the silence stretched out between his son and him, Matthew tried to think of some way he could volunteer himself. But to commit to practices, as well as games, was more than he could manage.

Surely saying no was better than promising something he couldn't deliver.

"I wish I could help you out, son. But—"

"Yeah. You have to work. I get it."

He sounded so jaded. Matthew felt both defensive and guilty. "It costs a lot of money to send you to Mountain View Academy. And to buy you and your sister all the latest—"

"I said *I got it,* Dad. You probably don't know enough about soccer to coach it, anyway."

That was true, which only made him more frustrated. "I'm sure I could learn."

"What's the point? You're too busy, remember?"

Matthew inhaled deeply. Reminded himself he was the adult here. "I'm sure you must be disappointed, but the soccer association will find you a new coach soon. Hopefully, one who actually understands the strategy behind the game."

"Yeah. Right." Clearly, Derrick wasn't holding out any hopes.

Matthew longed to say something that would make his son feel better. But there was no quick fix to this situation. Not for any of them.

"I'll phone the president of the soccer association and see what their plan is."

"Don't bother." Derrick hung up, as miserable as he'd been at the beginning of the call.

Matthew was left with the knowledge that he'd disappointed his son yet again. He sighed, then pocketed the BlackBerry, this time making certain to turn it off first.

He met Jane on her way out and could barely contain his disappointment. "I thought we might have a second drink."

"One was enough for me. And don't worry. I covered the bill."

Her gaze barely skimmed his face before she glanced away. Why was it so darn hard to get her to look him square in the eyes these days?

And he hated that she'd paid for their drinks.

He fell into step beside her as she headed back to the office. "This was supposed to be my treat. You know what that means?"

She raised her eyebrows questioningly.

"I pick up the tab next time."

"Next time?"

"Damn right next time." He let himself touch her elbow as they crossed the street. It was all he could do to let go of her once they reached the other side.

"Jane." He stopped her before she entered the revolving door that led to the lobby of their building.

"Yes, Matt?"

Ever since his phone call she'd been so cool and distant. He wished he could make up the ground that had been lost.

"I'm glad we had this talk."

Her expression softened. "Me, too."

"And we *will* do it again. Right?"

She hesitated. "Maybe."

And then she quickened her pace and disappeared into the building. He watched and wondered what she would have said if he'd told her the truth.

That Gillian thought they'd been having an affair because during one of their arguments he'd admitted that although he wasn't having an affair with Jane, he was more than halfway to being in love with her.

CHAPTER FIVE

ON WEDNESDAY EVENINGS from seven to ten, Gillian taught drama at night school and Matthew went over to her house to take care of the kids. When he and Gillian had split up, Violet had been only two. Much too young, Gillian said, to be away from her mother at night. So while Derrick could spend every second weekend with his father, Matthew was able to see his daughter only on day visits.

The trouble with that was that he never could be the one who helped her with her pj's, who tucked her in and sang her lullabies. Now she was almost too old for that, which only made the routine all the more precious to him.

Last summer, when Gillian had told him about the teaching opportunity, he'd jumped at the chance to look after the kids on that night. Now, every Wednesday, Matthew was able to be a part of his children's everyday life. Exactly what he wanted—and missed—the most.

On this Wednesday, Matthew read three of Violet's favorite books to her, then made her a snack of sliced apples and cheese.

Derrick was out with his friends. According to the note Gillian had left on the kitchen table, he was supposed to be home by eight to do homework. Matthew checked his watch. It was ten to now. He glanced out the front window.

Hurry home, Derrick. He was eager to see his son and discuss the soccer coach situation. He'd been talking his dilemma over with one of the young lawyers on staff, who was also a father with kids who played soccer. Tim had suggested he work out a team coaching arrangement with one of the other parents. That way, if work interfered with a particular game or practice, he'd have some backup.

Matthew wanted to ask his son what he thought about the idea. If Derrick seemed keen—hell, if he seemed mildly supportive—Matthew planned to start working his way through the team phone list to find a coaching partner.

"I'm s'posed to brush my teeth now." Violet had finished her snack and was gazing up at him with her huge blue eyes.

He scooped her into his arms and carried her toward the bathroom.

"I can walk, Daddy. I'm a big girl." She slithered from his arms and scampered ahead of him. Once there, he helped her to squeeze a tiny bit of paste on her princess toothbrush.

She set to work, brushing vigorously, while with her free hand she held on to his shirt as if to prevent him from going anywhere. He wished she didn't have to worry, that she would know she could count on him being here whenever she needed him.

During those first months in his own apartment, after he'd moved out of the house he'd shared with his family for thirteen years, the hardest times had been coming home from the office. Every night he would open the door to silence. Only, in his mind, he would hear the sound of running footsteps and little voices calling out, "Daddy! Daddy's home!"

Derrick had been beyond that stage by the time of the breakup, but not Violet. Matthew remembered setting down his briefcase so he could scoop her into his arms, and the giggles when he placed her on his shoulders and galloped around the dining-room table.

Gillian had claimed he was a workaholic, but there had been happy times, too. He wished that instead of letting his work drive a wedge between Gillian and him, she could have helped him understand how much he was missing.

But blaming Gillian for his obsession wasn't fair. His father's untimely death wasn't responsible for his compulsive work ethic, either. According to his mother, he'd always been an A-type personality.

When he had a job to do, he felt like he was in a tunnel. He couldn't focus on anything but the deadline in front of him.

His brother Gavin couldn't understand. But then Gavin was one of those guys born to be a dad. Even though he, too, had a demanding job, as an architect, he'd had no trouble fitting in lots of time with his twin girls.

And Gavin's life hadn't been a picnic. First the mother of his girls had deserted them. Then, when the twins were in first grade, one had been killed in an accident on the street.

For the sake of the daughter he still had, Gavin had relocated his small family to New Hampshire, where he was now happily remarried.

Whenever Matthew was in a pinch with his kids, he always asked himself what Gavin would do. Now, as he settled Violet into her bed precisely at eight o'clock and Derrick still hadn't shown up, he found himself once again wishing for his brother's wisdom.

Violet had always been a sound sleeper, and her eyes were closed by the time he had her covered. "Sleep tight, sweetheart," he whispered. He kissed her cheek, then left her room with the door ajar.

The view out the front window was disappointing. No sign of Derrick. He called his son's cell phone—last year's Christmas gift—only to be put through to messages.

"It's after eight, Derrick. You should be home by now. Please call as soon as you get this."

Matthew riffled through the newspaper, but he couldn't concentrate. An ad for watches caught his eye. Wasn't that the same brand Jane wore? He felt a rush of pure sexual desire as he pictured the gold band slipping up and down her slim, elegant wrist.

He imagined pressing a kiss to her wrist, then trailing

his mouth along the length of her arm until he reached the delicate skin of her neck. Would she moan? Sigh? How did Jane react when she was aroused?

He stopped the fantasy before it could go further. He had no right thinking of her this way. No right to wish for anything more than the possibility that they could be colleagues again. Friends.

He located the remote control for the television and cruised through the channels, finding nothing that could hold his interest. Resisting the urge to phone Jane, he started to pace.

The door to Gillian's bedroom was open, and as he walked by, he noticed a pair of men's shoes on the floor.

He paused. It was none of his business. He knew Gillian had been dating. But was the guy also spending the night?

For Matthew not to go into the bedroom to look around took a lot of willpower. He was especially curious about the master bathroom. Would there be an extra toothbrush in the holder? A razor and some shaving gel?

He didn't begrudge Gillian a sex life. But what impact would it have on the kids when their mother's boyfriend showed up at the breakfast table? Violet was too young to think much about it, but Derrick would understand what was going on.

The last thing Matt wanted was to start a fight with Gillian. But he would ask her about this, he decided. Surely he had some rights as a father.

His concern about Gillian's boyfriend faded, though, as another fifteen minutes went by and Derrick still wasn't home.

There were some numbers by the phone, and he recognized the names of two of the boys on Derrick's soccer team. He called both of them, but neither of the mothers who answered had seen Derrick this evening.

Hell. Now what?

Matthew was considering phoning Gavin, or even Nick, whose connections on the police force might be useful right about now, when finally the back door opened.

"Derrick." *Thank God.*

His son kicked out of his runners, then headed for the fridge without saying a word, or even glancing in his direction.

Don't jump to conclusions, Matthew counseled himself. It was what he imagined Gavin's advice would be if he were here. Keeping his tone calm and reasonable, Matt pointed out to his son, "You were supposed to be home forty-five minutes ago. Did something happen?"

"I missed the bus." Derrick poured himself a tall glass of juice.

"You missed the bus," he repeated. Did Derrick know how lame that sounded? Or perhaps that was the point. "Maybe you should have showed up at the bus stop five minutes earlier."

"Yeah. Maybe."

Matthew couldn't help it. His anger rose. "At the very

least, you could have phoned." He checked the impulse to say that he'd been worried, that he'd even been thinking about contacting the police.

"The batteries in my phone were dead."

"Really?"

"Yeah." Derrick's eyes met his and they were so full of defiance that Matthew knew he was lying. As if to prove it, his son's cell phone let out a burst of music, signaling an incoming call.

The chime repeated four times. Derrick ignored it. He was still staring at Matthew as if daring him to do something. Options ran through Matthew's head, most of them out of the question. He didn't want his first words to be spoken in anger. He struggled for calm.

One. Two. Three.

"You were supposed to be home by eight, Derrick, and you weren't. You don't have a good reason, so there will be consequences."

Derrick smirked.

Again Matthew had to rein in his temper. "You're grounded for the rest of the week—and that includes no cell phone." He held out his hand until his son passed it over. "Plus you won't see any friends this weekend."

His words hit their mark. The pressure on his chest eased as uncertainty flickered in Derrick's eyes.

But a moment later, the arrogance was back. "Fine. Ground me. Mom won't stop me from going out."

"I wouldn't be so sure about that." Matthew was so disappointed he was practically choking on it. He'd been thinking about the conversation he wanted to have with his son all evening, and none of this had been part of the script.

He cleared his throat. Tried to make a fresh start. "Now, about your soccer situation—"

"If you're talking about the coach, don't worry about it. Like you said, the soccer association found us a new one."

Damn. Could nothing go right for him and Derrick tonight? "Good," he said weakly. "I guess this means the game on Friday is a go."

"I guess." Taking the glass of juice with him, Derrick disappeared into his bedroom.

Matthew groaned with frustration, then picked up the newspaper one more time. He'd read through the business section and sports by the time Gillian arrived home.

She entered through the back door, too, and set down a bag stuffed with what looked like a batch of test papers. She'd taught drama between acting gigs before they were married, but she'd never really loved the work. It was something she did for the extra cash and to get out of the house.

She glanced around the kitchen, her eyes alighting on the plate he'd used for Violet's snack.

Feeling as if she'd caught him out, Matthew grabbed the plate and stacked it in the dishwasher. "How was class?"

"Not bad. I've got a decent group this semester. Some of them even have talent." She bent over to move

Derrick's sneakers out of the way. "Did Derrick finish his homework?"

Matthew felt his shoulders tense. "I'm not sure, but I doubt it. He wasn't home until almost nine. He's been in his room with the door closed since then."

Gillian rolled her eyes, as if this was nothing new to her. "I wish you would talk to him."

"I did. I told him he was grounded for the rest of the week." He remembered the men's shoes in her room. "By the way, is your boyfriend staying the night now?"

"What?"

"I saw a pair of men's dress shoes in your bedroom—"

"You were in my bedroom?"

"I was walking *past* your bedroom."

"Whose shoes are on my bedroom floor is none of your business, Matt. Or who is in my bed, for that matter."

"When it comes to my kids—"

"This has nothing to do with Derrick or Violet."

"I don't want strange men spending the night."

"Bruce doesn't spend the night, okay? He's a doctor and he works shifts, and sometimes he needs to shower and change after we've gone out."

His ex was dating a doctor. That stopped Matt cold. Of course, he'd assumed that eventually Gillian would move on with her life. But what bothered him was that his kids had a new man—a permanent man—in their lives.

"How long have you been seeing him?"

"That's not any of your business, either. I don't ask you for an accounting of your dating life."

"Well, maybe you should." Matthew was about to elaborate, when Derrick walked into the room. As earlier, he headed for the fridge.

"Derrick. Your father tells me you were home late."

"Yeah. He *grounded* me," Derrick said, as if it were some kind of joke.

"I don't understand why you find that so funny."

Derrick just shrugged and looked at his mother. Then he grabbed a soda from the fridge and left again.

"That kid," Matthew muttered. "You better watch that he sticks to the grounding I gave him."

"Really, Matt. And how am I supposed to do that?"

"Tell him to come straight home after school, that's how."

"And when he shows up at six, saying he missed the bus? Or at seven because he had to stay late to work on a school project?"

Matthew wondered how long these problems had been going on. "I guess you'll have to pick him up after school and drive him home."

"That easy, huh? And what about Violet? Nursery school ends at three-thirty, the same time Derrick gets out of classes. How am I supposed to be in two places at once?"

A movement from the hallway caught Matthew's attention. He realized their son hadn't gone to his room, after all. This was the moment of truth. He had to prove to both of them, to Gillian and to Derrick, that he was serious.

"Then I'll pick him up." He made his way to the front door, pulling his car keys from his pocket. When he passed his son, he patted his shoulder. "See you tomorrow, Derrick."

As he let himself out, he heard him mutter, "I'll bet."

JANE HAD GONE FROM NEVER being around Matthew Gray at all, to running into him several times a day, and it was proving to be hell on her composure. Midafternoon on Thursday she went down to the Cookie Tray, a kiosk next to the deli, hoping a heavy hit of sugar would help her through to dinner. Matthew was in the line ahead of her. All he ordered was black coffee.

"I admire your willpower," she said as she stepped up beside him. "Two cookies for me, please. And a large coffee with room for cream."

"How you stay so slim with that cookie addiction…" He shook his head.

"It's my new health club membership."

"You said you only use it for the hot tub and the sauna."

She shrugged. "Blame job stress, then."

"Speaking of which, have you got a minute?"

She checked the time. "Maybe two."

"Let's grab a table. We need to talk."

He had no idea, she was sure, how his words filled her with anticipation.

Undoubtedly, he wanted to discuss work, but the

reason didn't matter. Just being around him was enough. Since they'd been assigned the Keller case, he'd been in her thoughts more than ever.

Did he feel the same way? She doubted it. He appeared calm and slightly distracted as he held a chair out for her, then settled himself across the table.

"How's your schedule for the rest of the day?" he asked.

The glasses that made him look scholarly were in the front pocket of his suit jacket right now. Without them he seemed…not sexier, but more approachable. She expected him to smile at her with easy familiarity, but instead he pulled out his BlackBerry and started pressing buttons.

She wished she had her cell phone to hide behind. Since she didn't, she focused on the white plastic lid on her coffee cup. The small opening was smeared with lipstick. She'd forgotten she'd applied the dark red shade this morning. "I have a meeting in fifteen minutes. Then I'm free. Why?"

"I thought it would be good to get Keller's wife's input this afternoon. Catch her alone while her husband's at work and the kids are at school."

"Aren't I supposed to be the lead on this case?"

"Sorry. I didn't mean to push."

"Besides, shouldn't we wait until charges are laid before we put too much time into this?"

"Normally, yes. But I have a feeling that in this instance being prepared will pay off. Especially if we need to check into Keller's history in Maine."

"I was thinking of doing exactly that," she admitted. "I'm not saying he's lying. But I got the feeling he didn't tell us the whole story behind his move."

"Agreed. If he's keeping some kind of secret, we'll be better off knowing sooner rather than later. Which is why I'd like to hear Leslie's side of this."

Jane considered his comment. They rarely put much time on the docket before charges were brought. But Russell had asked them to pay special attention to this case. Finally, she nodded. "Okay, I'll talk to his wife. Did you want to come along?"

"I'd like to but I can't. I'm off to court now, then I'm driving to Mountain View Academy for three-thirty."

He didn't usually pick his kids up from school. And he seemed worried about something. "Is Derrick in trouble?"

"He was late home last night, so I grounded him."

"Sorry to hear that." In the past Matthew had been proud of his son's good grades and positive attitude. Was typical teenage angst causing these new problems? Or was this yet another repercussion of Matthew and Gillian's divorce?

"Yeah. It's a worry, all right. Not to mention a damn inconvenience. The drive to and from West Hartford will cut my afternoon in half."

"If it's Leslie Keller you're worried about, don't be. I can handle that interview on my own."

"Thanks, Jane." Matthew tucked away his Black-Berry and stood. "I'd better get to court now. Fill me in later, okay?"

"I will." Before going back to the office, Jane wanted to get some breath mints. She went to the small convenience store at the far corner of the office tower and selected a roll of peppermints. On her way to the till, she noticed her reflection in one of the security mirrors angled on the ceiling.

Her cheeks were pink and her eyes were shining like a schoolgirl who'd just been asked out by the grade twelve quarterback.

She was a professional, for heaven's sake, yet she'd never felt less like one. She had to get a grip on herself. If she couldn't learn to work with Matthew Gray, to treat him like any of her other legal colleagues…

Her thoughts were interrupted as someone deliberately stepped up to the counter beside her.

"Jane, I'm so glad I've bumped into you," said Eve Brandstrom. "We need to have a little chat."

CHAPTER SIX

WITHOUT QUESTION, Eve, in her designer suits and impossibly high heels, was the most stylish lawyer in the firm. She had an attitude to match—confident, poised and polished. Just her presence could sway a jury, and despite their years of working together, Jane felt a little intimidated by the older woman as she subjected her to a frank appraisal.

"Are you feeling all right, Jane?"

"I'm fine." She fumbled in her purse for money, then dropped it on the counter in exchange for the mints.

"I assume you were just talking to Matthew."

"Did you run into him in the lobby?"

"I didn't need to. Your expression is…revealing."

Jane's hand trembled as she tucked the package of mints into her purse. "Thank you," she said to the clerk. Eve followed her out of the store, then pointed out a bench situated in a corner of the lobby.

"Why don't we sit and chat for a minute."

"I have a meeting—"

"This won't take long. And it's important."

Feeling cornered, Jane followed her mentor to the bench and sat reluctantly on the edge of it. Eve settled back in her seat, crossed one leg over the other, then smiled.

Jane allowed herself to relax slightly.

"You know, Jane," Eve began, her tone confiding, "when I was a little girl and told my father that I wanted to be a lawyer and work at his firm one day, he didn't approve. He said it was too distracting for men to have women at the office."

"That's an old-fashioned viewpoint." Jane was willing to bet Eve's father hadn't objected to female receptionists and secretaries.

"I know. But at the time it was the prevailing one." Eve leaned a little closer. "In all the years I've worked at Brandstrom and Norton I've made it a point to prove my father wrong. To show that a woman can work with men without letting her emotions—or her sex drive— get in the way."

"I appreciate that, Eve. But are you suggesting that I haven't done the same?"

Eve sighed. "We're friends as well as coworkers, so maybe we should stop pussyfooting around the subject. Did your…relationship…with Matthew have anything to do with his divorce?"

"Of course it didn't."

"Don't forget, I was in the restaurant that day. I heard every word Gillian said."

"His marriage was already on the rocks. I was the scapegoat." Matthew had reassured her on that point, for which she was very grateful. "Despite what Gillian thought, Matt and I were having a business lunch."

Eve's dark eyes were piercing, but Jane didn't blink as she stared the other woman down. Finally, Eve let out a long breath. "Okay. I'm glad you told me that. I'd hate to see personal issues between the partners mess up the great working atmosphere we have at the firm."

"I understand."

"Especially where you're concerned," Eve continued. "You know I've always taken a great interest in your career. You have an excellent legal mind and an impressive presence in a courtroom. In many ways, you remind me of myself in my younger days."

"I appreciate the vote of confidence, Eve. I love working at Brandstrom and Norton."

"That's good to hear." The older lawyer stood. "I won't hold you up any longer. I myself have an engagement I'm running late for."

They split off, going in separate directions. *That went well,* Jane told herself as she made her way to the elevators.

But if that was true, why was her finger shaking so badly she could hardly press the up button?

AN HOUR LATER, on the drive to the Keller residence, Jane rehashed her earlier conversation with Eve and tried to reason out why she'd found it so upsetting. In her own way, Eve was being as sexist as her father. But Jane had to admit that what disturbed her the most was knowing Eve had been absolutely right about her suspicions.

Maybe not technically. Jane and Matt had never had an affair. Heck, they'd never even touched each other inappropriately.

But she did have feelings for him. Feelings that just didn't belong at work. Never in a million years would Jane have chosen to fall for a colleague. Yet that was exactly what had happened.

She was crazy about Matthew. For over a year she'd struggled with these feelings. She'd tried denial. She'd tried avoidance. So far nothing had succeeded.

Now what?

Work harder, Jane. Bury all your personal desires and disappointments and focus on your clients.

Maybe this wasn't the best course of action in the world. But it had gotten her through other rough patches in her life. Difficult breakups. The long illness and death of her mother. Then her dad's remarriage and abrupt disappearance from her life.

Following the instructions on her GPS, Jane ended up in front of a pleasant family home in the same neighborhood where Matthew's family lived. She parked on the street, then paused to mentally prepare for meeting Mrs. Keller.

Wally and Leslie Keller had been married for fifteen years. They'd moved to West Hartford from Maine last August, and had a son, Daniel, who was thirteen, and a daughter, Emily, who was eight.

Mrs. Keller did not work outside the home, and Jane

hoped to be lucky enough to find the coach's wife in this afternoon. She hadn't wanted to phone ahead, as that would have given the woman too much time to think and worry…and possibly invent stories.

Jane stepped out of her car and assessed the neighborhood. The Kellers' house didn't stand out from the others on the block in any way. The lawn needed mowing, but so did several of the neighbors'. She made her way to the front door, where she halted to listen before knocking.

Though the front window was open, all she heard was silence. If Leslie Keller was home, she wasn't listening to music or watching television.

Jane rapped on the door and waited what seemed a long time. Finally, the door was opened cautiously. A woman peered out as if expecting the worst. She eyed Jane nervously.

"Mrs. Keller?" she asked. When the woman nodded, Jane introduced herself. "I'm Jane Prentice from Brandstrom and Norton. Your husband recently retained—"

"Yes, yes, come in." Leslie Keller opened the door wider, then closed it swiftly once Jane was inside. Wally's wife was shorter than Jane by several inches. Her hair was combed but not styled, and she was dressed for housework.

Jane noticed the vacuum cleaner plugged in and waiting in the center of the adjoining living room. But it hadn't been on when she'd knocked at the door.

"I'm sorry to disturb you, Mrs. Keller, but I was

hoping you could spare me a few moments to discuss your husband's case."

The woman's cheeks paled, but she nodded. "Yes. Please sit down. Can I get you something to drink? I could make coffee."

Sensing the woman would calm down if given something to do, Jane nodded. "Coffee would be wonderful."

"Let's sit in the kitchen."

Jane followed her down the hall to the back of the house. The fridge was covered with a huge calendar filled with family commitments. "Soccer practice" and "Soccer game" figured prominently in many of the squares.

As Jane had guessed, Leslie Keller visibly relaxed as she set about the familiar routine of starting coffee to brew.

"How do you like your new house?" Jane inquired, settling on a stool across from the sink.

"It's lovely. Bigger than what we had in Bangor."

"And the neighborhood?"

The corners of Leslie Keller's mouth tightened again. "Our neighbors were welcoming when we first moved in. The kids had no problem making friends."

"But things have changed in the past week?"

"They definitely have. No one talks to Wally or me anymore. It's like we're invisible. You'd think someone would call. Offer some support. But we're new around here, and the Boutin children were born in this community. I guess I'm not surprised who people would choose to believe."

"It must be difficult."

Tears sprang to Mrs. Keller's small, tired eyes. "Especially for the children. Emily came home yesterday to tell us that all the girls in her class had been invited to a classmate's birthday party except her."

"I'm sorry. Kids can be very unkind and thoughtless."

"The birthday girl's mother is the one who addressed the invitations," Mrs. Keller pointed out.

"How about Daniel? Is he still playing soccer?"

"He doesn't want to, but his father is making him. I don't think it's fair. It's difficult enough for Daniel at school."

Jane sensed there was more to this. "Has there been any trouble?"

"Daniel's teacher phoned me yesterday. Daniel was overheard threatening to punch out one of the boys in his class." She threw up her hands. "Daniel's never been violent. Yet he admitted he said it. And that he was ready to do it. His father asked him why, but he wouldn't say. Of course we know. That boy must have said something about Wally."

Jane readied her notebook and pen. "Do you have the name of this boy?"

"The teacher didn't mention his last name, but his first name is Derrick."

Jane froze. Then copied down the name, even though she wouldn't forget it. Could this be Matthew's son? Surely not.

On the counter, the coffeepot had finished dripping,

but Leslie Keller paid no attention to the full carafe. She sank onto the stool next to Jane's, and her entire body seemed to cave in on itself.

"We never should have moved here."

Jane waited a beat before asking, "Why did you?"

After a hesitation the other woman said, "Because of Wally's work. He was offered a new opportunity with the company. The promotion was too good to pass up."

The explanation sounded smooth, almost pat. But Leslie hadn't maintained eye contact as she delivered it. "Was there another reason your family wanted to leave Maine?"

Leslie Keller seemed to be weighing options. Jane smiled sympathetically, hoping she would trust her. But all Mrs. Keller did was shake her head. "We moved for Wally's work. It was a smart career decision."

Jane used the probing expression that she usually reserved for the witness stand. "I hope you're being completely open with me, Mrs. Keller. Remember, I'm on *your* side. The police won't be."

The woman's face grew pinched at the mention of the police, but she didn't back down. "My husband is innocent, which means that girl is lying. Wally would never hurt a little girl. We have a daughter…Emily is only eight. How could anyone think Wally would do something like that?"

Jane had no answer to offer.

"You have to talk to Sarah Boutin," Leslie begged. "Explain to her how serious this is. She'll ruin our lives if she doesn't tell the truth."

"We can't speak to Sarah yet, Mrs. Keller," Jane explained. "If the police do bring a case against your husband, we will have full access to the evidence against him then."

"So now we just sit and wait?"

"Mostly, yes. But the police won't. You can be certain that even now they are investigating not only your husband's past, but yours, too, and your children's. If there were any problems or conflicts, they'll surface."

Leslie Keller stared into her coffee cup, not adding a word. Yet Jane's intuition told her that she was struggling with a decision.

Tell me! Jane wanted to cry out. But her mental telepathy didn't work. Leslie Keller remained silent.

When she left fifteen minutes later, Jane was certain that the Kellers were hiding something. Whether it would prove to be important, she had no idea.

AT THREE-THIRTY SHARP Matthew parked down the street from his son's school. He got out of the car and waited. Seemingly hundreds of kids spilled out the front door before he saw a familiar one.

It took him a moment to place the face, and then he realized the boy was Daniel Keller, the soccer coach's son.

He looked dejected, and Matthew felt for him. Matthew wondered how much the boy's parents had told him, and hoped that it had been everything. For sure the kids at school wouldn't protect him.

As he had that thought, Derrick emerged from the school along with three other boys from the soccer team. They didn't take long to notice Daniel, and as they moved toward him, a sick feeling rose in Matthew's gut.

He started running toward Derrick and his pals, but he was too far away to get there before they closed in around Daniel. Dialogue ensued, but Matthew couldn't make out the words, only a taunting tone. He could tell the boys were roughing Daniel up, but when they finally dispersed, there was no obvious injury. Daniel stood, his face red, hands clenched at his sides, as his so-called teammates ran off ahead of him.

Derrick stopped short the moment he spotted his father. Matthew glanced from his son to Daniel, then back again. "Want to tell me what's going on here?"

Derrick shrugged, then, bypassing him, started toward the car. Matthew checked the urge to ream out his son there and then. He'd deal with Derrick later. Turning to Daniel, he asked, "Are you okay?"

The kid hesitated. "Yeah."

"Need a lift home?"

Daniel looked over to where Derrick stood waiting by the locked sedan. "I don't think so." He hitched his backpack higher on his shoulders, then brushed past Matthew.

Matthew wanted to tell him that he was sorry. That Daniel didn't deserve any of this. That life was unfair and that he should try not to take his teammates' behavior personally.

But most adults couldn't deal with this kind of bullying. How could anyone expect an adolescent to cope?

His heart heavy, Matthew returned to the car and stared down his son before unlocking the doors so they could get in. Once inside, he paused before starting the ignition.

"I can't tell you how disappointed I am in you right now."

Derrick kept his head averted. "No kidding."

"What I just witnessed you and your friends do to Daniel... Where did you learn to act that way?"

"TV? Violent video games?"

Matthew gritted his teeth. God help him, he could understand why some parents resorted to physical violence with their children. He drew in a lungful of air and prayed for patience.

But he couldn't find any. How could his son—a boy who used to cry if he accidentally stepped on an ant— be capable of such cruel behavior?

Ganging up against anyone was wrong. But Derrick had picked on a boy from his own soccer team. A new kid in school who hadn't had time to make the good friends who might have stood by him at a time like this.

Matthew began driving, giving his son some time to reflect. As he passed the turnoff for the house, Derrick said, "What are you doing?"

"We're going to Daniel's, and you're going to apologize."

"But Daniel won't be there yet." There was panic in Derrick's voice.

"We'll wait."

"Mom's expecting me."

"I'll call her and explain."

Finally seeing his father's determination, Daniel sank back in his seat. The way he set his jaw and crossed his arms reminded Matthew of his brother Nick.

Matthew parked out front of the Keller home, then used his BlackBerry to call Gillian. She didn't sound pleased, but eventually agreed that their son ought to stay and apologize.

After that, Matthew and Derrick sat in silence. Matthew was still too angry to give Derrick the lecture he deserved. After about fifteen minutes, Daniel ambled into view. His head was downcast, so he didn't notice them until it was too late to run.

"Daniel." Matthew left the car, went up to the boy and put his hand on his shoulder. "Are you sure you're all right?"

He nodded stiffly, not quite meeting Matthew's eyes.

"My son has something he needs to say to you. I hope you're willing to listen."

He didn't reply. But at least he didn't take off. Matthew turned to his son. Derrick was out of the car but keeping his distance. He looked belligerent, but a little embarrassed, too. Dared Matthew hope Derrick felt ashamed?

Come on, son. Do the right thing.

Matthew waited, almost aching to hear an appropriate apology emerge from his son. Derrick was angry, but he wasn't really a bully.

Was he?

The silence between the two boys was becoming unnerving. Finally, Derrick stepped forward. "Daniel," he said, but before he could go any farther, a car drove up and double-parked by Matthew's sedan.

Gillian was at the wheel, with Violet in the booster seat behind her.

"Mom?"

A moment later Gillian was on the sidewalk, reaching for her son's hand. "Come on, Derrick. I don't want you hanging around here."

"He was just about to apologize." Matthew was so livid he could hardly keep his tone civil. What was Gillian doing? He'd told her what had happened. Why was she undermining him like this?

"*You're* the one who owes *us* the apology." Gillian's gaze skimmed past Daniel without acknowledging his presence. "To me and to our children. To the entire community, for that matter."

"What are you talking about?" The situation was spiraling out of his control. "Get your hands off Derrick. Our son needs to—"

"He needs to come home," Gillian interrupted. "Right now. I don't suppose you've told him."

Told him what? Matthew almost said. But in that instant he knew what this was about. Gillian must have found out he was representing Wally Keller. Probably someone from the soccer team or the parent of one of Derrick's friends had called her soon after he had.

"I can't believe you would stoop so low." Gillian

jabbed her index finger toward him. "Defending pedophiles. Putting your career ambitions before the safety and security of your own children."

"Gillian, for heaven's sake…" How could she talk this way in front of the boys?

At the mention of *pedophile* Daniel had taken off. The front door opened and Matthew caught a glimpse of Leslie Keller before she whisked her son inside.

Matthew wondered how long Wally's wife had been standing by the door. Had she heard Gillian's rant?

Damn. He would never get his son to apologize now. He turned to Derrick, who was staring at him as if he'd just transformed into some sort of monster.

"Is it true, Dad? Are you really Coach Keller's lawyer?"

Matthew pushed the hair from his forehead, suddenly hot and frustrated. This was not the way he would have chosen to broach this topic. "Could we go back to your place to discuss this, Gillian?"

But she'd already marched their son to the passenger door of her car. Once Derrick was inside, she faced Matthew again. "I don't think that would be a good idea at all. I can't stand to be anywhere close to you."

A moment later she was in the car and had restarted the engine. As Matthew watched Gillian drive away, Violet raised her hand and waved.

CHAPTER SEVEN

MATTHEW OPENED the glass door of the Corner Diner and stepped back into his past. The fat burgers on the grill, the familiar faces of the people who worked here, the classic rock music playing on the sound system were all as comforting as home.

When he was a teenager, he'd hung out here with his friends. So had Gavin and Nick. Though all three Grays had long since moved out of the neighborhood, they still met here occasionally.

If there was one place Matthew could relax and be himself, this was it. Already, as he crossed the room, heading for his brother's table, he was loosening his tie and undoing the top buttons of his starched white shirt.

Nick lounged at a table near the window, still in uniform, his upper body stiff with the regulation bulletproof vest he wore under his short-sleeved shirt. He'd chosen a chair that faced the door, and though he appeared at ease, Matthew knew he was keeping a close eye on all the comings and goings—one of many habits he'd picked up in his ten years on the Hartford police force. On track for a promotion to detective, Nick was more serious about his work than ever.

"Hey. How's it going?" Matthew slid into the chair opposite his brother's. It was hard not to miss Gavin at moments like this.

Matthew and Nick loved each other—no question about that. But growing up, their temperaments had sparked like oppositely charged ions, especially once their father had passed away. Nick was independent and rebellious and didn't take kindly to his oldest brother filling the role of head of the household in the family.

Not that Matthew had been keen to do so. But their father's death had hit their mother hard, and he'd had no choice.

The professions he and Nick had chosen had only exacerbated their adversarial relationship. The cop and the defense attorney. Not a combination made in heaven.

Over the years Gavin had mediated between them. It was thanks to Gavin that Sunday dinners with their mother had been civil, if not downright enjoyable, most of the time.

Those Sunday dinners were something else that had suffered in Gavin's absence. Now weeks could go by before either he or Nick organized anything. That Matthew only had access to his kids every other Sunday didn't help.

"Life is good. You?" Nick had a mug of coffee in front of him, as well as one of the diner's famous thick milkshakes. It seemed that no matter how much he ate he retained his fit, muscular physique.

"*Good* would be stretching things."

Nick raised his eyebrows but had no time to question him. A server—someone new, Matthew hadn't seen her before—arrived for their orders. She was in her late teens, maybe early twenties, and all the while Matthew was telling her what he wanted, she was making eye contact with his brother.

Nick's popularity with the opposite sex alternately amused and annoyed Matthew.

Today he chose to be amused. "Do you tip them ahead of time?" he asked after she'd left for the kitchen.

"Wouldn't you like to know."

"Honestly? No. My life is complicated enough."

The hard blue of Nick's eyes softened a little. "Are the kids okay?"

"Violet's a doll, as always. But Derrick…" He relayed a condensed version of the previous night's events.

Nick was obviously concerned. "Picking him up from school is a good idea. This is the age when boys can really get into a lot of trouble."

Thanks, bro. Just what I needed to hear.

"Do you know his friends?"

"A few of the ones on the soccer team."

"Well, that's where I would focus my energy if I were you. Let him and his friends use your apartment as a place to hang out."

"How do I get them to do that?" Just getting Derrick to visit was hard enough, even on the weekends when he was supposed to be with his father.

"Keep a supply of snacks and frozen pizzas on hand. The latest video games. Whatever it takes."

"That might have worked a few weeks ago. But Derrick's really angry at me right now, and probably his friends are, too."

The server returned with their burgers and fries. "Can I get you anything else?"

Was it just his imagination, or had she sounded hopeful as she'd said that? His brother grinned and shook his head. "We're fine for now, Cindy."

Matthew waited until she'd left. "Cindy? I didn't notice a name tag."

"You should pay more attention to pretty women and less to menus." Nick inhaled a portion of his burger. "Back to what we were talking about. Why is Derrick pissed? Is it still the divorce?"

"Probably that, too, but what really has him and Gillian upset is that I've agreed to represent his former soccer coach. A guy named Wally Keller."

Matthew could sense his brother's defense mechanisms slipping into place. As long as they were discussing family matters, he and Nick were okay. But work was one of the sensitive topics they tried to avoid.

"What're the charges?" Nick's tone remained casual, yet his eyes were once again focused.

"No charges yet. But one of the sisters of a player on the team has accused Keller of sexual assault."

Nick sucked in his breath, then swore. "How old's the sister?"

"Twelve. Same as Derrick. She and her brother are

twins." Before Nick could explode with righteous anger, Matthew held up his hand to stop him. "I know what you're thinking, but consider this from the coach's point of view. He says he didn't do anything wrong. He's adamant about that. Even you would have a difficult time not believing him."

"That's what they all say." In disgust, Nick set down his unfinished burger.

"False accusations are made sometimes. The guy deserves—"

This time it was Nick who put up a hand for silence. "Don't start down that road. You know where it leads. We both do."

Matthew acknowledged the truth with a nod. He couldn't blame his brother for being cynical about the justice system. Cops worked their butts off to prepare cases against the criminals they caught in the streets. The vast majority of the suspects who ended up in court were guilty. Yet defense attorneys—like Matthew—often got them reduced sentences, or off completely.

"Most of the parents from the soccer team have sided against Keller. As far as I can tell, Gillian is one of the more vocal ones."

"Can you blame her? If my son's coach was suspected of sexual interference with a minor, I'd be pretty damn upset, too."

He wasn't surprised that his brother would think this way. Still, it hurt. "I never thought I'd see you siding with Gillian against me."

"That's not fair."

"There is such a thing as innocent until proven guilty."

"That's what you always say."

Because it's the truth. Matthew didn't bother uttering the words. What was the point? He and Nick had been running through permutations of this argument ever since he'd gone to work for Brandstrom and Norton. And it was one argument that neither of them would ever win.

BY THE TIME MATTHEW arrived home it was dark. The apartment had a stale smell, masked slightly by the lemon products the cleaning crew used. They'd been in today, he could tell, because his shoes were lined up neatly in a row in his closet.

He threw his jacket and briefcase on the padded bench, kicked off his shoes, then added them to the lineup. After stopping in the kitchen for a beer, he made his way to the big-screen television.

His home was a lot more comfortable since he'd asked Gavin's wife to help him decorate. The paint job and new furnishings had put a dent in his savings, but the money had been well spent.

He slipped a disk into the DVD player, then made himself comfortable on the coach and flicked through the menu before choosing one of his favorite *X-Files* episodes. The opening credits had just ended when his BlackBerry rang.

The phone was still in his jacket pocket and he

wanted to ignore it. But what if Derrick was trying to get in touch with him?

With a tired groan, Matthew rolled up from the couch and loped to the entranceway. His heart rate spiked when he recognized Jane's number.

He jabbed the talk button. "Hello?"

"Matthew? Are you at the office?"

"Just got home, actually."

"Oh. Sorry to bother you. I was going to fill you in on my interview with Leslie Keller. But it can wait until tomorrow."

She was right. It could. But he didn't want it to. "I'd really like to know how that went. Any chance you could stop by for a drink? I'm having one now."

"After the day I've had, I could use a drink. But I'm driving."

"I'll send you home in a cab," he promised. "That way you can have more than one."

"That's probably not a great idea. It's a work night, you know."

"We'll get more done tomorrow if we get up to speed tonight. Besides, we can compare notes about our rough days." That would give them plenty to talk about. He waited, hoping she would agree.

"Oh…all right. What's your address?"

It turned out she wasn't far away. He'd just uncorked some wine and pulled out a block of aged cheddar when the intercom buzzed. He hit the button for the security lock, then went out into the hall to greet her.

Jane was almost always immaculate in her dress and

grooming, so he couldn't help but be surprised when she stepped off the elevator. Her suit jacket was unbuttoned, her blouse rumpled, and she had dark smudges under her eyes that he suspected might be from old makeup. She must have been rubbing her eyes. Or crying? Surely not.

She noticed his reaction. "I warned you I had a bad day."

"Hey. Did I say anything?"

"You didn't have to. Your elevator has mirrors. I know how I look."

Beautiful. At least, in his opinion. But he didn't want to scare her off. "You've put in a long day."

"Not only that, but I had a run-in with Eve after I left you this afternoon."

He didn't like the sound of that. "What about?"

She shook her head. "I need fortification before I get into that story."

"One glass of wine coming up." He paused for her to go through the doorway first, then followed, helping her to remove her jacket, then taking her bag and setting it on the bench next to his briefcase.

"Collapse on the sofa," he invited her. "I promise it's comfortable. I'll be right back with the wine." When he arrived with two glasses, she was still standing in the middle of the room.

"You're a fan of the *X-Files*." On the TV screen Mulder and Scully were engaged in one of their classic arguments about the limits of science.

He turned down the volume. "Guilty as charged."

"I own the complete collection, too." She glanced around the room. "Impressive, Gray. You have rugs and art and lamps and stuff. When did you find the time to do all this? I've lived in my condo for three years and the walls are still bare."

"My sister-in-law helped. Allison's an interior designer in New Hampshire." He handed Jane the glass of wine, then went back for the cheese plate.

"Helped?"

"Okay, she did everything. But she e-mailed me pictures before she bought, so I had the final approval."

"I don't suppose she'd consider decorating my place, too."

"I could ask her. But she and Gavin are already pretty booked. They've set up a business together, and of course they have Tory to keep them hopping."

"You said Tory's doing okay. Losing my mother when I was already an adult was hard enough. I can't imagine losing a twin sister at such a young age."

"Thank God kids are so resilient." He hoped his were, as well. Violet's smile had been so sweet when she'd waved at him from the car today. With any luck she hadn't heard any of the garbage Gillian had spewed out on the street. Bad enough that Derrick had been there. Gillian was drawing their son into a conflict that was way too grown-up for him to handle.

As if Jane knew what he was thinking about, she picked up the photo of his children he kept on the coffee table. "Very cute."

"That was taken last Christmas. They've changed a

lot since then." He'd have to arrange for a new photo soon. Gillian used to handle that stuff, and she probably still did, but he doubted that she would be providing him with copies from the photographer anymore.

"Everyone says children grow up so fast." Jane replaced the photo and sipped her wine.

He studied her face. She'd relaxed a little, but not much. He wondered what her opinion was on the subject of children. "Do you plan to have kids?"

He'd voiced the question casually, but he was keenly interested in her answer. If starting a family was something that mattered to Jane, he wanted to know.

She didn't take long to reply. "No. Definitely not."

"You sound pretty sure about that. Don't you like kids?"

"Yes, but I doubt if I'd be very good with them. I've never been around children much. Unlike you, I was an only child. In high school I used to work in my dad's landscaping business, helping him with the books, so I never got into babysitting the way some teenagers do."

There was more behind her answer than that. He could sense it. "You don't know what you're missing, Jane."

"Obviously not." She smiled, but tightly. "Hey, aren't you curious about the meeting with Leslie Keller?"

"Sure." He could take a hint, and willingly went along with the change in subject. "You found her at home?"

"I did, and she was alone, which was another lucky break for me." Jane sipped more wine, and her watch slid down her arm. Distracted as always by the movement, he took a moment to process what she'd said.

"Did you ask her why they'd moved from Maine?"

"That was one of my first questions, and she gave me the same line we got from Wally."

"Was she more convincing than her husband?"

"Not at all. I still feel there's more to the story than they're admitting."

Despite Matthew's fatigue, his investigative instincts kicked in. "We need to know what happened."

"I did my best to convince Mrs. Keller of that. I warned her the police would be investigating and that she was only tying our hands by concealing the truth."

"And—?"

"And nothing. She wouldn't talk. But I could tell there was something, Matt."

He trusted her gut feel. "I'll call Wally tomorrow. Hopefully, he'll be more forthcoming than his wife. Either way, we should do some research in Maine. Interview past employees, neighbors, the kids' teachers…"

"Might be better to wait and see if charges are laid."

"Do you really think so?"

She sighed. "No. You and I both have a hunch the Kellers are hiding something. The sooner we find out what it is, the better."

"Good. Now. Tell me what happened with Eve."

The lines of tension returned to Jane's face. "She caught up to me right after I left you, and pulled me aside for a little heart-to-heart."

He had a bad feeling about this. "What did she want to talk about?"

Jane looked up at him. "You."

CHAPTER EIGHT

Now Matthew *really* didn't like the sound of this. "Why did Eve want to talk about me?"

"She was curious to know if I had anything to do with the breakup of your marriage," Jane said.

"What? That's none of her bloody business."

"Maybe that's why she waited so long to ask me. Eve and I are friends as well as business colleagues. She's concerned about my future. That's all."

"Well, I hope you told her you had nothing to do with the divorce. Hell…I can't count the number of times you offered to do more than your share at work so I could leave earlier to be with my family."

"Yet you never did."

"I know." He stared into his glass and swirled the burgundy. "If I had those years to do over, I'd change a lot of things. For one, I'd have made getting home for dinner a bigger priority."

"Why didn't you?" she pressed.

"It's complicated, Jane. I used my work to mask the issues Gillian and I had at home. Plus, I love my work. Always have."

He felt driven to be number one at whatever he did. He wasn't clear why. Partly, it was his personality. Maybe becoming de facto head of the household at sixteen had played a part.

"But when the relationship between you and Gillian began to seriously deteriorate, you still didn't change."

"You're not letting me off easy, are you?"

"I'm sorry. I should just butt out."

"No. These are valid questions. Ones I've asked myself many times. Gavin was always giving me the same good advice that you did. Go home. Spend time with your family."

Matthew slouched into the soft cushions as he thought back to those days. "Much as I wanted to spend time with my kids, though, I dreaded the fights with Gillian. My stomach would churn at the prospect of going home to her. I not only stayed late to finish my work…I invented reasons to stay later than required."

He glanced at Jane, expecting to see disapproval. But she only looked sad. "You said Gillian wasn't interested in counseling?"

"Actually, we did go one time, right after that episode at the restaurant. But the session was a failure. The counselor told me later that he felt Gillian had already checked out of the marriage, emotionally speaking. I suppose that in many ways I had, too."

He laughed, suddenly self-conscious. "You're going to start feeling like a psychiatrist. I don't know why I keep crying on your shoulder like this."

"Maybe because we're friends."

Their eyes met, then they both glanced away. Jane reached for some cheese. He finished his wine and went for the bottle in the kitchen.

He took a minute to compose himself. He had no doubt why Jane had made that comment about being friends. She was reminding him of the boundaries of their relationship. Already her reputation at Brandstrom and Norton had suffered thanks to him. He could just imagine the talk at the office should they become romantically involved.

He couldn't do that to her. It wouldn't be fair. He had to get past this feeling of attraction…and connection. Could he walk the tightrope between friendship and desire?

He had to.

Returning to the living room with bottle in hand, he asked lightly, "Ready for a top-up?"

She held out her glass, and he could tell that she, too, had used the past few minutes to get a grip on her emotions.

"So. Tell me about *your* day. You said it was tough. Did you pick up Derrick from school on time?"

Matthew had to hand it to her; she couldn't have chosen a less romantic topic if she'd tried. "Yeah, I was on time. So on time I witnessed an incident I would rather not have."

He told her about the bullying and about his attempt to have his son apologize. "It ended up an absolute disaster. Gillian is furious that I'm handling the Keller case, and I'm sure she'll turn Derrick against me, too."

"That's just…appalling. I mean, I can understand Gillian having reservations about you taking this case."

He nodded, knowing Jane was right. The moral and ethical dilemmas defense attorneys faced almost every day were something that garnered precious little sympathy from the public. In theory almost everyone could agree on an accused's right to be presumed innocent until proved guilty, and to have a trained lawyer as his advocate.

But in practice…well, that was something else.

How could you defend someone like that? was something he'd heard far too often in his career already.

"It's unfortunate she had to express her views in front of Derrick, though," Jane continued.

"Not to mention Daniel. Poor kid. I can just imagine what he's been through this past week."

"Talk to your son. Explain your side of the situation."

"I will, but it's not as if he and I don't have enough issues. Besides, I worry that Gillian's tirade is going to feed Derrick's bullying behavior." Matthew was still deeply disappointed in his son about that. And frustrated beyond belief at not having the support of Derrick's mother in dealing with it.

"There is one way out of this mess," Jane said.

"Yeah?"

"You could drop out of the case."

Her suggestion drove all other thoughts from his mind. "What?"

"If it's going to make more problems for you and

your son, maybe you should walk away. I can handle this on my own."

"I already tried to do that, remember? You're the only one with the time to handle lead on this. And I'm stuck as official hand-holder, thanks to Wally's request."

"But if you explained about Derrick…"

"I did that," he reminded her. "And you saw how sympathetic Russell was. Besides, now that I've started, I can't back out. I've given Wally Keller my word. His wife and children are counting on me, too."

"You're not saying you don't trust me to handle this, are you?"

"God, no. You're a terrific lawyer, Jane. But the both of us made a commitment to our firm and to our client. And I think we've got to see the case through."

"No matter the cost?"

"I love my children. But they are not going to vet my cases for me."

"Would you still feel that way if you knew Coach Keller was guilty?"

The question she was asking was right out of a university ethics course, but the situation was all too real this time. "No. Of course it wouldn't. I'd still believe that Keller was entitled to a fair trial and a competent defense."

She looked at Matthew speculatively. "You do think Keller is innocent, though, don't you? You seemed to find him very persuasive when we met with him."

"I know not many guys accused of what Coach

Keller is accused of will admit it. But, yeah. I did think he was sincere when he said he was innocent."

"You don't believe he's capable of putting on an act?"

"To some extent, yes. Like you, I'm pretty sure the Kellers are hiding something that happened in Maine. And that raises my suspicions just a little."

But he still wanted to believe the guy was innocent. Not just because Keller had been kind to Derrick, although that was part of it.

Jane finished her wine in one long swallow, then carried her goblet to the kitchen. He heard the tap running. A moment later she returned with a glass of water. She leaned against the wall, took a sip, then pressed the cold glass to her forehead.

"Jane?"

"For now, I'm going on the assumption that he's innocent. Tomorrow I'll call someone to do some preliminary legwork in Maine. And hope that whatever the Kellers are hiding, it has nothing to do with our case."

"Good plan."

The room fell silent and Matthew knew that at any moment Jane was going to say that she should be leaving. Only, he didn't want her to leave.

He liked having her here.

She was exhausted after her grueling day, yet she still looked beautiful to him. He wanted so badly to touch her. Any part of her would do.

Her silky, long hair. The side of her face. Her neck…

His gaze met hers. Could she tell what he was

thinking? She probably could. He saw an element of pleading in her soft brown eyes, as if she was begging him not to cross the boundary she had so carefully placed between them at the beginning of this case.

If only they weren't partners in the same law firm, he wouldn't have to worry about lines of any kind.

Of course, if they hadn't both chosen Brandstrom and Norton, they never would have met.

"It's really late."

Jane's voice was husky. Because she was tired? Because of the wine? Or maybe, just maybe, she was feeling the same attraction he was right now.

"Would you please call that cab, Matt?"

He kept looking at her for a few moments longer. *Don't go,* he wanted to say. *I need you.*

"Please, Matt," she repeated, breaking away and heading for the washroom.

When she returned a few minutes later, he'd already placed the call. She smelled fresh and her face was brighter, as though she'd splashed it with water.

"The cab should be here in five minutes." He walked her out to the hall, then rode down with her to the lobby. In the elevator they stood with at least two feet between them. Though they weren't touching or looking at each other, he could still feel a pull toward her.

As the doors slid open, he could see out the glass doors of the building to the Yellow Cab waiting at the curb.

"Great, the taxi's here already. Good night, Matt. Thanks for the drink. And the company."

He nodded, not trusting his voice. No sooner had she left than he started anticipating the next day in the office.

As he rode the elevator back up, he wondered if his determination to stay on this case wasn't because he believed it was the right thing, but because he wanted to keep working with Jane.

JANE WENT TO WORK the next day determined to avoid Matthew if possible. Going to his apartment the previous night had been a mistake. Oh, they'd followed all the rules of polite society. Not once had either of them behaved inappropriately.

But when they'd ridden down in the elevator together, the sexual tension had been so high that one look, one touch, would have set her off.

And she didn't think she was the only one who had felt that way.

What she needed was one full day devoid of any encounters with Matthew whatsoever.

But as luck would have it, when she stepped into the main-floor elevator at twenty past eight, Matthew was one of the two men already there. He seemed well rested and cheerful.

"Good morning." He made room for her to stand next to him.

"What are you so happy about?" She removed her sunglasses and stowed them in her purse. Though she'd had only two glasses of wine, she'd awoken with a headache. Also, she'd been out of coffee and the bread had gone moldy. She was hungover, tired and hungry.

On top of all that, Matthew had the nerve to appear absolutely gorgeous.

"I thought we proved something important last night," he said quietly so the man sharing the elevator couldn't overhear.

"Such as?"

"That we can work together and keep things professional."

Was he crazy? He'd spent the evening looking as though he might tear her clothing off at any second. And she'd been guilty of wishing he'd do exactly that.

"Are you saying you didn't want—"

"Oh, I wanted a lot of things." His breath warmed her cheek as he spoke. "And I still do."

Her nerve endings danced at the suggestion.

"But the point is, I didn't act on those feelings."

"True." But how much longer did he expect their willpower to last?

The elevator doors opened and the other man got off. Seemingly reluctant—maybe he *had* overheard their conversation and was curious to know how it would end. Well, so was she.

They resumed their ascent to the twenty-eighth floor. As soon as the doors began to separate, she moved forward. "See you later."

He pressed the open button to hold the doors, then followed her. "How about two o'clock?"

Her resolution to avoid him completely was getting shot to hell. "Can this wait until tomorrow?"

"Afraid not. I had a call early this morning. Naomi

Little is the mother of one of Derrick's soccer mates. She's asked us to drop by while her children are still in school. I'm not sure what she plans to tell us, but it could be important."

"Fine." Jane tried to tear her gaze from his, but there it was again. The look that told her he longed to touch her. If she alone felt this way, she wouldn't be so worried. As the situation stood, however, she was very concerned.

She finally turned away and strode to the end of the hall, to her office in the unobtrusive location that she'd selected for the express purpose of avoiding accidental meetings with Matt.

Now she was running into him all the time, and it was just as difficult as she'd feared.

She cared about her job. She'd worked damn hard to earn her partnership, and she didn't intend to start over again at another legal firm. As she slid behind her desk, she acknowledged one simple fact.

If she and Matt had an affair and it didn't work out, her reputation would suffer the most.

Matt thought they'd proved something last night, and so did she. Unfortunately, they differed significantly on *what* they'd proved.

Forget about him, she told herself. *It's time to focus on work.*

She had a backlog of e-mail and phone messages to attend to before a luncheon meeting with one of her clients. When she returned to the office at one o'clock, a message waited from the private investigator she'd called earlier.

She dialed him back right away. "Liam? It's Jane Prentice from Brandstrom and Norton."

"It's been a while, Jane. Keeping busy?"

"Very. I need some background on a new client. He and his family moved here in August from Bangor, Maine."

"We've got a good operative in Maine," Liam assured her. "Tell me what you need."

She filled him in as much as she could, including their hunch that the Kellers were omitting significant details that could influence the case against the husband.

"If something happened out there, we'll get to the bottom of it," Liam promised her. "Now that business is taken care of, tell me about you. Married yet?"

She laughed. "Still single. And planning to stay that way."

"Big mistake, Jane. Just so you know, my offer still stands. You don't have to commit right away, though. We could start with dinner. Tonight."

Liam was a flirt, but she knew that if she said yes, it would happen. She hesitated, tempted. If she was dating someone else, the situation between her and Matthew might be neutralized.

But she wasn't interested in Liam romantically and she liked him too much to use him that way.

"Maybe next time," she said, keeping her tone light.

"You're such a tease."

She hung up the phone with a smile on her face. And just at that moment Matthew appeared in the doorway to her office.

CHAPTER NINE

"IS IT TWO ALREADY?" Jane dipped her head, pretending to study her watch in order to mask her reaction to Matthew's unexpected appearance. The racing heart. The suddenly damp palms. Why did her nervous system keep betraying her this way?

"Who were you talking to on the phone?" He sounded like a jealous lover. Even the glasses he wore with such style couldn't mask the intensity in his blue eyes.

"Liam James. If the Kellers had any secrets back in Maine, he'll find them."

Matthew didn't seem appeased by her explanation. "It sounded like he was flirting with you."

She folded her hands over the papers on her desk and raised her eyebrows. "And if he was…?"

"You're saying it's none of my business." He strolled to her credenza, where he picked up the picture of her cat. The snapshot was a recent one, taken by the tree this Christmas past. Polly was wearing her new red collar.

Most of her colleagues had photos of their children on display in their offices. Jane had Polly, and she made no apologies for that. Everyone needed someone to love.

Matthew placed the picture frame down gently. "And you're right, of course." He moved closer, placing his hands just inches from hers and leaning toward her. "But I don't like the idea of you with another man, Jane."

Now he was plain making her angry. They had established rules, the two of them, and he kept breaking them. "Back off, Matt. You have no right talking to me that way. I'm free to flirt with, or even date, whomever I choose."

He set his mouth firmly, but he did as she asked and moved away from her desk. "Is that what you want to do? Date Liam?"

"Don't be an idiot." She got up from her desk and slipped on her blazer. She felt Matthew watching, and knew he noticed the buttons across her chest strain with the maneuver.

Ignoring how that made her feel, the pulse of awareness, of raw sexual attraction, she did up her jacket, then grabbed her briefcase. "Shall I drive this time?"

He hesitated.

"It's my turn," she pointed out.

"You're not giving me an inch today, are you?"

"Not even a quarter of one."

"Should be an interesting afternoon. Okay, your car. Let's get going."

ONCE THEY WERE ON the road, Jane said, "Tell me more about this woman who called you. Her son is on the soccer team?"

Matthew patted his seat belt to make sure it was secure. "Pardon? You were looking in the other direction when you asked that."

"I was checking the road."

"Well, maybe you shouldn't talk when you're changing lanes." He did when he was changing lanes, but it was different when you were the passenger, he was discovering. He eyed the traffic light ahead, and tensed as the green gave way to yellow. Would she try to…?

Jane pressed on the accelerator. Yes, she would.

"I was just asking how well you know Naomi Little."

"Not well at all. I've seen her at the games and she was at the party at the beginning of the season," he recalled. "But not her husband."

"What about her son? Is he one of Derrick's friends?"

"Not a close one. Jared is new to the team this year, like Daniel. Derrick described him as a 'brainiac.'" Matthew grimaced. "Like being smart is a bad thing."

"Derrick's smart, too."

"You wouldn't know it from his grades lately. He used to love books when he was little. He was always watching those science shows on TV and pestering me to read to him." Now those days were a distant memory.

Maybe if Matthew had been around the house more Derrick wouldn't have stopped those good habits. Matthew rubbed his forehead and wondered whether making up for those kinds of mistakes was possible.

Gavin assured him it was. He hoped his brother was right.

Jane merged smoothly onto the freeway and Matthew felt himself relax a little. She really was a good driver, and soon they were in West Hartford.

Like most families whose kids were on the team, the Littles lived within blocks of Gillian and the children. Jane slowed so they could pick out house numbers.

"There it is," he said.

She stopped the car in front of the nicest home on the block. He whistled.

"This could be a photo spread in a decorating magazine," Jane agreed. "Can you imagine how much time it must take to keep the lawn and gardens so immaculate?"

"They probably hire a landscape service." Unlike the residence across the street, he thought, as he glanced at the neighbor's tired-looking two-story colonial.

Matthew got out of the car and waited for Jane to join him on the sidewalk. They went up the main walk together, and the front door opened before they were close enough to knock.

Mrs. Little was dressed in a light gray pantsuit more appropriate to the office than a day at home. In the background the television was playing. The show sounded like a soap, to Matthew. And was that a hint of wine on Mrs. Little's breath as she smiled at them?

"Thank you for coming, Matthew."

"Nice to see you again, Naomi. This is my colleague Jane Prentice. She's the lead lawyer on the case."

"Oh?" Naomi eyed her speculatively. "Well, please follow me. We can talk in the living room."

She invited them to sit, then disappeared for a moment. The television noise ceased and she returned with a tray of tea and homemade cookies. After a little polite banter, Matthew realized he would need to take control of the conversation or they would end up spending hours and accomplishing little.

"When you called, you mentioned being concerned about the allegations against Coach Keller."

A concerned frown replaced Naomi Little's social smile. "Most of the parents on the team are really angry with him. And part of me is, too. But my husband and I feel Wally's getting a raw deal."

"You don't believe he's guilty?" Jane pressed.

"I can't say for sure, of course. But he struck us as such a genuinely nice man. He made a place on the team for Jared, even though our son had never played the sport. And he put in extra time helping him develop some of the basic skills of the game—something I really appreciate because Jared's dad doesn't have time to play sports with him very often. He works in international finance and travels a lot."

Matthew felt a familiar stab of guilt. He hadn't had the time to play sports with his son, either. Hadn't *made* the time, he amended. He added going to the park and kicking around a soccer ball to his mental list of activities he planned to do with the kids this weekend.

"The police have a statement from Sarah Boutin,"

Jane pointed out. "Do you have any reason to suspect Sarah may not be telling the truth?"

Naomi's eyes clouded at the suggestion. "I don't doubt something happened to that poor child. She's changed a lot recently—anyone can tell. She used to be outgoing and cheerful."

Matthew was surprised to hear this. "Have you seen Sarah lately?"

"I see her all the time. The Boutins live across the street. Sarah went back to school yesterday, so at least she's recovered enough to do that."

Matthew glanced out the window at the house that had struck him as neglected. "Is that the Boutins' home?"

"Yes. The property is really getting run-down since the children's father moved out."

"We were told the Boutins had recently separated," Jane said. "Do you know when this happened?"

"Just after Christmas, I'm afraid. The whole family seems to be falling apart. They were such nice, quiet people. Now I hear cars coming and going, and doors slamming, in the middle of the night. I'm not sure what's going on over there, but one thing is for certain. Claudia Boutin's social life has been a lot more active since her husband moved out."

"Interesting." Matthew exchanged glances with Jane. Sarah and Robert were too young to have friends visiting them that late at night. So who was doing all the driving?

He would have loved to go next door to question Claudia. But the Boutins were off-limits, not only to Wally right now but to Wally's legal counsel, too.

"Please let us know if you notice anything else suspicious," he told Naomi on their way out, and she assured him that she would.

On the way to the car, Matthew eyed the Boutins' front window. "Interesting," he said to Jane. "They're the only ones on the block with their curtains drawn."

AFTER LEAVING the Little residence, Matthew suggested he and Jane grab a coffee at a local café and compare their impressions. Twenty minutes into their discussion, Jane glanced at her watch.

"Isn't it time you picked your son up from school?"

He'd been making notes and he stopped midsentence, jolted by a feeling of panic. How could he have forgotten about Derrick? He checked his own watch. Twenty-five after three.

"Cripes! What was I thinking?" He gulped the rest of his coffee, then shoved his papers back into his briefcase. Too late, he realized he had a problem. "I don't have my car."

"We can use mine."

She hadn't hesitated before offering, but he sensed she wasn't keen on accompanying him. Unfortunately, he couldn't come up with another option.

"Thanks a lot, Jane. I owe you."

He hurried outside, Jane right behind him. The May afternoon was warm and the interior of Jane's car had become unbearably hot. As soon as she had the engine started, Jane lowered the windows, then glanced at him.

"So where are we going?"

He gave directions to the school, glad now that she drove on the speedy side. Tension became anxiety as he wondered what mood Derrick would be in this afternoon. Matthew would have liked to think that his son wouldn't behave rudely, but these days Derrick's behavior was something he just couldn't predict.

Kids were already streaming out of the building when they drove up to the school. Jane found a place to park about a block from the main exit, and he quickly opened his door.

"I'll go find him." He paused, then added cautiously, "I feel I have to warn you…he's been a little snappy lately."

"That's okay," she said, but her expression was apprehensive. She really didn't want to be here, and he shouldn't have put her in this situation in the first place.

But there was nothing he could do about that now. He searched the sea of adolescent faces, trying to pick out his son. The first person he recognized was Robert Boutin. There was a girl beside him. His twin sister, Sarah.

He had to agree with Naomi. The girl had changed. From the soccer games, he remembered a bright, attractive girl. A tomboy with confidence and sass to spare.

But the young woman walking with her brother now displayed none of that verve. Despite the heat, she wore a loose, long-sleeved top. Her skin was sallow and her eyes lacked their usual spark. She clung to her brother's side and she cringed when any of the other kids got too close.

For the first time since he'd taken the case, Matthew felt doubt. Had he done the right thing by agreeing to represent Coach Keller?

The kids were heading in his direction, and a moment later Robert recognized him. He acknowledged Matthew with a nod. "Mr. Gray."

There was mistrust in Sarah's eyes as her eyes met his, and his feeling of unease grew. This child was so clearly suffering. She hadn't had an easy time of it. First, the breakdown of her family unit; then, her father moving away. Finally, this.

Someone had abused this child. If not Wally Keller, then who?

"Hi, Robert, Sarah. Have you seen Derrick?"

"He's still inside," Robert said. "Should be out soon. Coming to the game tonight?"

"You bet. It's time for the team's luck to change."

"I sure hope so."

Robert and Sarah continued on their way, and Matthew went back to monitoring the crowds. He wondered if he might spot Daniel Keller again, but he didn't. Eventually, Derrick showed up with the same group of guys he'd been with yesterday.

"Derrick," Matthew called, raising his hand so his son could find him in the crowd.

He wasn't surprised when Derrick scowled at hearing his voice. But what did surprise Matthew was hearing Gillian right behind him.

"Matthew? What are you doing here?"

CHAPTER TEN

"WHAT DO YOU MEAN, why am I here?" Matthew said. "You asked me to pick up Derrick from school this week because you were busy with Violet."

But their daughter wasn't in her usual seat in the back of the car.

"Where is she?"

"I asked a friend to take her home from nursery school today. Do you think I would trust you with either of the kids after what you've done?" Gillian waved at their son. "Derrick! Over here!"

To Matthew's consternation, Derrick headed straight for his mother. Matthew's instinct was to grab his son by the shoulder, but he fought against it.

"This isn't the plan we agreed to."

Gillian glared at him. "We made that plan before I found out about your newest client. I suppose it's your business if you want to defend child molesters. But it's my business to protect our children."

Under his breath, Matthew counted to ten. Gillian had her good qualities and he truly believed in general that she was a loving mother. But when she lost her temper about something, passion overrode her good sense.

Fine for her to condemn him for taking this case.

But talking this way in front of Derrick was plain wrong.

He looked at his son. Derrick now stood close to his mother, clearly signaling whose side he was on. Only, it wasn't right for him to be in the position of choosing sides. Couldn't Gillian understand that?

"Derrick, please get in the car while your mother and I discuss this."

Derrick waited for his mom to nod before trotting to her car and climbing in the passenger side.

Matthew lowered his voice to barely a whisper. "You think you have to protect them from *me?*"

"From your values, anyway. I have a call in to my lawyer. I'm asking him to review the custody arrangements in light of your current…activities."

"Cripes, Gillian. This case doesn't affect my ability to be a good father."

"When have you ever been that?" She narrowed her eyes as she glanced beyond him. "Is *that woman* with you right now?"

Prickles crept up the back of his neck. "If you're talking about Jane Prentice—"

"She is. I'd recognize her anywhere." Gillian's anger mounted. "And you had the nerve to deny that the two of you were having an affair."

"I said that more than a year ago," he pointed out. "And now my personal relationships are none of your business. However, since you seem so keenly interested, Jane and I are working on a case together."

Gillian's lips curled into a sneer. "She's defending him, too?"

Matthew didn't answer.

"Why am I not surprised?"

"Leave her out of this."

"Wow. How chivalrous."

He stepped away from her. "Gillian, I know I haven't been the best father. I'm trying to change, though. If you really cared about Derrick's and Violet's best interests, you might be more supportive of that."

"Have you thought about what Derrick is supposed to say to his schoolmates when word gets out what you're doing? When the case goes to trial, this is going to be all over the papers."

"Slow down, why don't you. Keller hasn't even been arrested and you have him as front-page news."

"It could happen," she insisted. "And what will you tell Derrick then?"

"The situation will be delicate," Matthew agreed. "But I'll talk to Derrick and explain why I have to do this."

"Great. Good luck with that, because you'll never convince me that this is something you have to do. You just want the publicity. The notoriety."

"Actually, Gillian, you have no idea what motivates me at work. You never have."

"Maybe not. But I do know when I need to protect my children."

"They are *our* children and I have rights, too. Don't you dare do this to me again, Gillian. I'm not going to stop spending time with Violet and Derrick. I'll be at the soccer game tonight and I'll be picking them both up Saturday morning as usual. And if you try to interfere again, then *my* lawyer will be calling *your* lawyer."

MATTHEW WAS SO ANGRY he was trembling when he got back into the car. Jane didn't say a word, just shifted into Drive and headed for the city. She didn't go to the firm, though; she drove to her condo and parked under the building in her usual space.

She shut off the car and sighed heavily. "That was pretty intense. You okay?"

"You heard?"

"The car windows were open," she reminded him.

He swore. "I'm sorry you had to witness that."

Trust him to worry about *her.* "I'm not the one you should be concerned about now. Does she often lose control like that?"

Jane didn't know Matthew's former wife very well. When his marriage had been falling apart—and when other men might have been unable to resist complaining to whoever would listen—Matt had never spoken a word against the woman.

Occasionally, Jane had encountered Gillian at company functions, but their exchanges at those had been minimal—polite chitchat at best.

The one time she'd seen evidence of Gillian's dark side had been last year during that ugly scene in the restaurant. Jane had given her the benefit of the doubt then. Though she'd been wrong, Gillian had thought her husband was having an affair. You couldn't blame a person for going a little crazy in a situation like that.

But Jane *could* blame her for going nuts in front of her son.

She had no idea how Gillian could say those things to Matthew in the first place. The woman had been married to a defense attorney; she ought to know the score. And then to speak so frankly in front of Derrick.

It was unforgivable.

"Gillian's always been volatile. I don't think I bring out her good side. Especially since the divorce."

"She doesn't seem to care if the kids overhear her."

"Yeah. No wonder Derrick's so angry. And Violet must be terribly confused." Matthew drew an uneven breath. "What the hell should I do?"

Jane had one idea, but she didn't think he would like it. "Let's go upstairs. We need to decompress before we head back to the office."

Matthew followed her into the building, up the elevator, to her condo. Polly was at the door as soon as Jane unlocked the dead bolt, meowing as desolately as if she'd been abandoned for days.

Jane bent to stroke her soft white fur, then made room for Matthew in the foyer. "Go through the hall and sit down. I'll be right back."

She poured him a cold glass of water and one for herself, then carried the glasses into the living room. Polly had sized Matthew up and pronounced him a pushover. She was already settled on his lap, dropping white hairs onto his navy wool trousers.

Jane passed Matthew one of the glasses and waited for him have a long drink before she asked, "Feeling better?"

He shrugged.

She sat on the sofa beside him. "Gillian's terrible, Matthew. Why didn't you tell me?"

"She's only terrible to me. She's actually a pretty good mother."

Jane couldn't believe that. Good mothers didn't put their children in the middle of disagreements with their parents.

She kicked off her heels and settled into the cushions. Now that she had seen the tactics Gillian was prepared to use, she was more concerned about Matt than ever. "I want you to reconsider dropping out of the Keller case."

Matt managed a twisted grin. "I had a feeling you were going to bring that up again."

"Seriously, Matthew. If Gillian's going to make your life hell, is it worth it?"

"You might as well tell me to quit being a defense attorney. I've taken the case. I've committed myself. Though I've got to tell you, I'm really hoping this is one time our client isn't lying to us. I'll feel a hell of lot better if it turns out Keller truly is innocent."

"And if he isn't?"

Matthew started to say something, then stopped. "Jane, do you remember when you first decided you wanted to be a lawyer?"

"Not really. I sort of eased into the career."

"How do you 'ease' into several years of undergrad work, then three years of law school?"

"Okay, I always knew I wanted to go to university, but I wasn't sure what I would study." That she'd just lost her mother after a long and painful battle with cancer hadn't helped. Her father hadn't been in any shape emotionally to offer her guidance, so she'd gone to one of the counselors at school.

"I took an aptitude test before college. Law was one of my suggested careers. I didn't think too much about it, and enrolled in general studies for my first two years."

"What made you decide to apply to law school eventually?"

"This will sound lame, but I had a boyfriend at the time who wanted to be a lawyer. He convinced me to write the LSATs with him."

"Which you aced," Matthew guessed.

She acknowledged this with a nod. She'd placed in the top three percent of students. "Yes, I did, and that gave me the confidence to put in my application. Obviously, I was accepted."

"What about the boyfriend?"

"Unfortunately, Brent didn't make it. He ended up switching to business administration. And switching girlfriends, too." Funny how she could summarize those times in a few simple sentences. The reality had been so much more complicated. And painful.

"His ego couldn't handle it, huh?"

"That was part of the problem. But that summer I had some health issues that didn't help the situation." A cancer scare. She'd been so afraid that what had happened to her mother was about to happen to her, too.

"Were they serious?"

"At the time, yes. But everything worked out fine." She couldn't tell him more than that. Not now. Even to this day she had trouble thinking back on that time without getting emotional.

Her mother had always said that the best way to deal with your pain was to focus on someone else. Jane often put this advice into practice, and now seemed like another perfect time for it. "What about you, Matt? When did you decide on the law as a career?"

"Shortly after my father died. He was such a healthy guy. His massive heart attack sent us all into shock. Mom coped by watching a lot of old movies on TV. One night she made all of us boys watch *To Kill a Mockingbird* with her. At first I thought it was kind of lame. But when the movie was over, I knew that when I grew up, I wanted to be a defense lawyer."

"I never watched that movie. But I loved the book. Scout was such an easy character to relate to."

"I connected more with Atticus. This sounds hokey, but I thought that if I grew up to be like him, I'd be able to take care of my mother and my younger brothers."

"That isn't hokey. It's admirable."

"Hey, I'm not trying to make myself out to be a

heroic crusader or anything. We all come into this profession with ideals, and eventually most of them are crushed."

"So true." You wanted to believe your clients were innocent and you were protecting them from injustice, but the truth hardly ever worked out that way.

"Still, I have to defend every client as if they were Tom Robinson. I know most of them aren't. Most are guilty to one degree or another. But I can't treat them that way. And I can't judge them. It isn't my role. It isn't *our* role," he added gently.

She was moved by his sincerity. And by the fact that he trusted her enough to talk to her so openly. "You're right. Our firm has a duty to defend Coach Keller. But as I've said, I could handle this one on my own. You don't have to be involved."

"I appreciate the offer. But I owe the guy one. And I gave him my word. You know as well as I do that his life is hell right now. The last thing he needs is one of his lawyers bailing out on him."

"Just because his life is hell doesn't mean yours has to be, too. Gillian clearly has no qualms about using this case to turn your kids against you."

"It won't be the first time she's tried to do that. I'll talk to Derrick about this after tonight's soccer game. We'll sort things out."

She doubted a solution would come that easily. And despite his attempt to reassure her, Matthew knew it. He was clenching his water tumbler so hard she worried the glass might shatter.

Polly must have sensed his tension, too, because she let out a disgruntled yowl, then pounced lightly to the floor, leaving a trail of white hairs behind.

"I'll grab a lint brush." With her penchant for black business suits, Jane kept several brushes in her home and one in her purse. She grabbed the brush by the front door, where she usually gave herself a final check before heading to work.

When she returned to the living room, Matt was standing, swiping ineffectually at the front of his trousers. She handed him the brush, and when he was done, instead of passing it back, he grabbed her hand.

"Jane? Thank you."

"For what?"

"For being a friend. For understanding. And listening. And knowing what I need."

She supposed he was referring to the way she'd brought him here instead of heading straight to the office. She looked into his eyes and felt a flood of empathy toward him. He'd taken the high road with Gillian last year in the restaurant, and he'd done the same thing today. Jane couldn't help but admire him and respect him.

But her feelings didn't stop there.

His hand on her shoulder felt hot. So hot it burned out any other sensation. She swallowed and shifted her gaze from his eyes to his mouth. He had such nice, kissable lips. A firm jaw and cleft chin.

Bringing him here had seemed like the only thing to do earlier. But she'd known it was risky. And now... She swallowed. If he would only stop staring at her so intently.

His eyes were burning into her, touching her soul and connecting in a way she simply could not deny.

Once, this man had been so off-limits.

Now, though, the situation was different.

Matt was divorced, for one thing.

And they were alone.

She and Matthew were never alone, not really. Even at work, in an office with a closed door, she was always aware that at any moment they might be interrupted or overheard.

That wouldn't happen here.

"Jane?"

There was urgency in the way he spoke her name. If ever she was going to back away, now was the time. But she didn't. Couldn't.

A second passed, and they were still standing there, only inches apart. He placed his fingers under her chin and levered her face up toward his.

And then they were kissing.

And it was good.

There was no first-kiss awkwardness. It felt natural and right. Yet why was she surprised? This was Matt and everything with Matt felt that way to her.

"I want you, Jane," he murmured into her ear. "You don't know how long I've wanted you."

His words were sweet and intoxicating, and they were all she wanted to hear.

Their kisses deepened. She tangled her fingers in his

hair and breathed in the aroma of his skin. Pulled tight against his body, she could feel that they would be perfect together. Everything about him felt so right.

If only they didn't work at the same firm.

I could leave.

But without the firm, she would be lost. If she had other interests, other friends... If she believed she and Matt really had a shot at making this work...

But she didn't. Not if she was honest with herself. She backed up slightly. "We have to stop."

His lips brushed her cheek, the corner of her eye. "Isn't this why you invited me up here?"

"No! Of course not." She stepped away from him, but he took hold of her hand.

"Be honest. Tell me you feel it, too."

She didn't dare tell him how much. "We work together."

"So do lots of other lovers, I'll bet."

Lovers. She wanted to think of them that way. But it just wasn't realistic. "Not at Brandstrom and Norton they don't."

"So this is about Eve and what she said to you?"

"Partly," Jane admitted. "I know you love your job, and so do I. Do you really want to jeopardize that?"

"Why would we? We're consenting adults. This is nobody's business but ours."

"If you're talking about what happens outside office hours, you're right. But could we really leave our feelings for each other behind when we go into work? I don't think I could."

"Well…after this case is over, we won't work together again."

"Remember what Davis said. The firm is too small to accommodate lawyers who can't work together. And consider your children. You probably didn't notice, but this afternoon Derrick looked at me like I was his worst enemy."

Matthew didn't say anything to that, but his lips tightened. "Don't get angry at him. He's just a child."

But she could tell that Matt *was* angry.

"It's Gillian's fault," he said explosively. "She's fed him all sorts of terrible lies about you."

"So I gather."

"Once Derrick gets to know you—"

"Do you think he'll let me close enough for that to happen?" The answer in Matt's eyes confirmed her opinion. She swallowed the hurt, the feeling that this was so *unfair.*

"Come here." Matthew's arms banded around her, giving her an illusion of security. Despite her reservations, she didn't have the heart to resist. She let her head relax against his chest, and listened to the agitated thumping of his heart. Inhaling deeply, she soaked up his essence, the scent that was uniquely Matthew.

Like his kiss, everything about being held by him felt right. She shivered as his lips skimmed the top of her head.

"After this case, Jane…"

She longed to believe. To hope. Instead, she mustered all her willpower and pulled out of his embrace.

"After this case, there will be another. And many more after that."

Matthew started to say something, then stopped. "I'd like to argue with you, but you're right. Damn it, I'm putting you in a terrible situation again. You'd think I'd have learned something after the last time."

She hated that he kept blaming himself about that. "It wasn't your fault."

"You're being too generous. As usual." He shoved his hands into his pockets and crossed to the other side of the room. "I'm sorry. I should have better self-control."

"Don't apologize for that kiss." She was glad it had happened. She couldn't pretend that she wasn't.

"You're amazing, you know that?" His eyes were so warm she had to glance away. "You're beautiful and smart. Warm and caring. How is it that you never married? Was it the boyfriend in law school? Did he hurt you too much?"

"That's part of it, I suppose. I had another relationship end painfully about five years ago. I guess I'm one of those people who are unlucky in love."

Desperate to change the subject before he challenged her glib comment, she picked up his empty water tumbler on the end table. "Would you like something else to drink? Or maybe we should head back to the office and grab a coffee on the way."

He ignored her questions. "I've noticed the way men watch you. Yet you never seem to return their interest. Why would that be?"

"Too busy."

"I don't think so."

"Care to review my billable hours this past year?" She slipped her heels back on and checked her makeup in the hall mirror before running a lint brush over her suit. "Ready to go?"

Matthew was still regarding her. "You're avoiding my question."

Yes, she was. And for good reason. As much as she trusted Matthew, she had one secret he would never know.

CHAPTER ELEVEN

HAVING SEPARATED FROM Jane as they left the elevator, Matthew retreated to his office with his large take-out coffee. Deliberately, he closed the door behind himself. He didn't want to be disturbed. He couldn't remember the last time he'd felt so stressed.

Actually, he could. It was the day he and Gillian had given up on their marriage. The morning had started with a huge fight, then culminated with Gillian kicking him out of the house they'd bought, renovated and lived in together for almost thirteen years. On that sorry day he'd ended up in this very office with a hastily packed suitcase and no idea where to turn next.

He felt much the same right now.

His son hated him almost as much as his ex-wife did. His work life was in chaos. And he was falling in love with the one woman he couldn't have.

Matthew slid behind the desk and took a long swig of the dark roast blend. Caffeine sometimes helped, but not today. The message button on his phone blinked relentlessly. When he reached for the receiver, though, it wasn't to check his calls but to place one.

He had the urge to connect with the family. First he dialed Nick, then his mother. Both were out. Gavin, however, answered his cell on the first ring.

"Matt? What's up?"

Matthew let out a huge sigh. Just hearing his brother's voice helped. Gavin had always been the calm one in the family. He was also a terrific father and had provided useful advice on more than one occasion.

"I'm worried about Derrick." He told his brother about the case he'd taken on and Gillian's reaction to it. Then about the bullying he'd witnessed. "I'm just so disappointed Derrick would behave that way. Clearly, it's my fault. I haven't been around enough to set the right example."

"Don't go blaming yourself. That won't help anything."

But Matthew noticed he hadn't really let him off the hook. "Okay. What *will* help?"

"Tell me what you think first."

"Well, he's got to apologize, obviously. I was also planning to have a talk with him, too. I guess I should have done that when it happened. But I was too angry to think straight."

"Understandable. In fact, it's probably better this way. You and Derrick were both too emotional at the time. Can you imagine going to court and presenting your closing arguments without any preparation whatsoever?"

Gavin's analogy made Matthew feel a little better. "Thanks, bro."

"One thing you might want to keep in mind, though."

"Yeah?"

"Derrick knows that what he did to Daniel was wrong. Chances are he's feeling really terrible about it. Give him a chance to redeem himself."

"Good point."

"And what about Violet? How is she doing?"

"She's great. I'm spending as much time with her as Gillian will allow." Remembering the one thing that was right in his life felt good. The tightness in his chest eased a little. "How about Tory? Is she excited about summer holidays?"

"Not really. She loves school and doesn't want it to end. She's worried about missing her friends." He laughed. "Man, it's great to have these kinds of problems now."

Matthew understood what he meant. After she'd lost her twin, Tory had gone through a frightening stage where she'd been unable to assert herself. Psychiatrists told Gavin she'd identified so much with her sister that she hadn't fully developed her own personality.

"You sound happy, too," Matthew said. Even more than usual, he thought.

"Well, we've had some big news this week."

Matthew could think of only one thing that would put that lift in his brother's voice. "Allison's expecting."

"You guessed it. She did the home test yesterday. We couldn't be happier. We're having a celebratory party tonight."

"Congratulations, bro. Give Allison and Tory a big hug from me." He'd send Allison flowers. He was very fond of his new sister-in-law, not the least because she made his brother so happy.

Losing Sam had been devastating for Gavin. There'd been times his brother had thought he'd never recover from the pain. But Gavin was strong, and so was Tory.

Knowing his brother's family was doing so well gave Matthew a measure of peace. He finished his coffee, then began to tackle the backlog of work messages. Soon he was lost in the problems of others.

He made notes on several files and became so engrossed in the details of one particularly complicated case that he didn't notice when someone opened his door and entered his office.

The sound of a throat being cleared drew his gaze up.

And there stood Jane.

His heart shifted to full throttle, mocking his earlier attempts to be calm.

"Just thought I would remind you about Derrick's soccer game," she said.

He checked his watch. "Cripes, where did the time go? I need to leave in the next ten minutes if I want to make it on time."

She already had her back to him as he got up from his chair. "Jane?"

She paused.

Her eye makeup was smudged again. Was she tired?

Or upset? The urge to pull her into his arms was overwhelming. Instead, he grabbed a tissue from the box he kept nearby for distraught clients.

"Hold still." He moved close enough to draw in her subtle scent, to feel the warmth of her body. Carefully, he dabbed at the gray marks on her skin.

She said nothing, not moving, almost frozen.

"I owe you an apology," he murmured.

"It's okay, Matt."

Despite her reassuring words, he could tell she was upset. "No. It isn't. I shouldn't have kissed you. Much as I enjoyed it, I shouldn't have gone there."

"To my place, you mean?"

"That, as well." He heard someone walk by in the hallway and felt Jane stiffen. "Who was that?"

"Eve. Just my luck." She backed away from him. "You shouldn't have done that, either, Matt."

"Done what?"

"Touched me."

"But you had something under your eye." He showed her the smudge on the tissue.

She shook her head. "You know what I mean."

And he did, of course. "I'm sorry. You're right. But, Jane, it isn't easy. All I want to do when I'm around you is touch you."

"Shh!" Her gaze flew back to the open door.

Maybe he was being indiscreet, but couldn't seem to help himself. "I need to talk to you about this. About how I feel."

"Not here."

"Then meet me after the soccer game. How about my place?"

She shook her head.

Maybe she didn't trust being alone with him. He named an Italian bistro close to her place. She shook her head again.

"Not a good idea, Matt."

"Jane."

He had a deep urge to touch her once more, but she slipped away before he had the chance. If not for the soccer game, he would have followed her, but seeing his son was just too important. He tossed a few papers into his briefcase, then closed his office door behind him.

As he strode along the hall toward the exit, he passed a few coworkers and greeted them absentmindedly. Several more were waiting by the bank of elevators, heading home for the evening. Eve was among them.

She held herself rigidly and made a point of skewering him with her gaze, her expression serious.

"How are you?" he asked, but she didn't answer. A short chime announced the arrival of the next elevator. He stepped inside, but Eve didn't. She was still glaring right at him as the door shut.

MATTHEW WAS PREPARED for Gillian to make trouble. She wasn't at the soccer field yet when he arrived, even though Derrick was getting ready for the opening kick. His son must have caught a ride to the field with one of his buddies.

Traffic had been light and Matthew had had time to pick up a burger. Standing on the sidelines, he unwrapped his dinner and took a bite.

Several of the other parents were already there, but not many acknowledged his presence. He supposed most of them knew by now that his firm had agreed to represent Coach Keller.

The new coach was out on the field with the boys. The father who had acted as coach at the last game was in the bleachers, and seeming happy to be there.

Matthew took stock of the players. His son was again with the boys who had ganged up on Daniel Keller the other day. Robert Boutin and Jared Little were kicking a ball back and forth, while on the other side of the coach, Daniel Keller stood all alone.

What a sorry mess. Matthew hated the way this ugliness had affected the boys.

When his burger was done, Matthew trashed the wrapper, then settled in the bleachers. He spotted Naomi Little, who smiled quickly before returning her focus to the field. She'd changed from her suit to designer jeans and a pink sweater. He tried to remember if he'd ever seen her husband at any of the games, but couldn't recall even one time.

The whistle sounded and the game began. Matthew followed the play intently, pleased for his son when he intercepted a midfielder, then passed to a team forward.

Despite his concentration on the game, Matthew could tell when his ex-wife arrived. He'd developed a sixth sense where Gillian was concerned. Or was he just being sensitive?

He turned, and sure enough, there she was. She had Violet with her, and as soon as the little girl saw him, she came running. "Hi, Daddy!"

His spirits lifted as he plucked her up and settled her on his lap. In another year or two she'd be too tall for him to do this. The thought made him sad, made him even more determined to maximize the time he spent with her.

He glanced over at Gillian, who had chosen a seat at the other end of the bleachers. She nodded stiffly, and he was relieved that, for whatever reason, she wasn't going to give him any grief right now.

Probably saving it all for later.

Well, he didn't care about that, as long as their children weren't witness to any of it.

As his daughter chatted about a new game she'd learned at nursery school, he found himself remembering the day Gillian had told him she was pregnant with their second child.

His excitement had been tempered by Gillian's ambivalence. She'd been on the verge of restarting her acting career and the pregnancy had meant she'd have to put her dreams on hold once more.

After Violet was born, he'd suggested hiring a nanny so Gillian could get back into the theater, but she'd refused.

He wondered if she regretted that decision. If they ever got to the point where they could have a civilized conversation, maybe he'd ask her.

A cheer rose from the spectators on the other side of the field when the opposing team scored a goal. The Blazers' dejection was obvious as they shuffled back into position for the goal kick.

Five minutes later, another goal was scored against them. His son's team had talent; they just weren't using it. They were disjointed, not playing as a team, and the new coach was part of the problem, Matthew thought. He didn't know everyone's name yet, and just keeping the right number of players on the field, filling all the required positions, seemed to be all he could handle.

Mercifully, after the third goal against them, the referee blew the halftime whistle. The players trudged in from the field, heading for their water bottles.

Matthew's eyes were trained on Derrick as another boy, the center fielder, walked up to him.

"Hey. Is it true about your dad?"

Derrick's shoulder's stiffened. "Yeah."

"What's the matter with him? Does he like perverts or something?"

Derrick lifted his head, and for a split second, his eyes met his father's. Then he turned back to the center fielder. "My father's an asshole. And I don't want to talk about it."

The two boys separated. The other boy had no idea that Derrick's words had been as much for Matthew to hear as for him. As the venom of his son's words spread through his system, Matthew felt a mixture of hurt and guilt and anger.

"Daddy? Why did Derrick call you that bad word?"

He'd been asking himself the same thing. But the answer was obvious. "I guess Derrick is angry at me. But he shouldn't have used that word."

"Why is he angry?"

This answer wasn't quite as obvious. "I think it's because Daddy and Mommy aren't living together anymore."

"Oh." Violet thought about that a moment. "I'm not angry at you."

Thank goodness for that. "Want to kick a soccer ball around for a bit, honey?"

Violet nodded. "I'll get the ball from Derrick's bag."

Once the break was over and they were heading back to the bleachers, Violet decided it was time to sit with her mother. Matthew walked her over to Gillian. His ex-wife's back straightened as he drew near. Her lips thinned and her eyes narrowed. Still, she managed a smile when Violet sat down beside her.

"Are you getting bored watching your brother?"

Violet nodded.

"I brought your coloring book. It's in my bag on the grass over there." Gillian pointed to a spot next to the bleachers.

As Violet ran to get it, the softness disappeared from Gillian's face. She finally looked up at him, acknowledging the fact that he hadn't moved. "Yes?"

"I'd like to drive Derrick home after the soccer game." With the score three-to-nothing, he doubted there would be a celebratory trip for Slurpees.

"Derrick has homework."

"It's important that I talk to him."

She shook her head as if trying to rid herself of something unpleasant. "Okay. Fine. Just don't be too late. I don't want him falling behind in his math."

"Thanks," Matthew said, though the word was hard to spit out. That he had to ask permission to speak to his own son was galling. On the other hand, he had to appreciate that Gillian had a handle on Derrick's schoolwork.

His son's team didn't do any better in the second half of the game, and after the final whistle a disappointed troop of boys made their way off the field. Matthew noticed that even in defeat, the boys avoided Daniel. He stood apart as the coach talked to the team, and was the last in line as the boys filed past the other team members to shake hands.

When the other kids left with their parents, Daniel alone wasn't offered a ride. Though Matt was worried that speaking to the boy would only make things harder for him, he felt compelled to ask Daniel if he needed a lift.

"Mom's waiting in the car down the block."

"Right." Matthew sighed heavily, then turned to his son. Derrick was making it clear that he was anything but overjoyed at the prospect of spending time with his father. They were the only two left on the field when Derrick finally stopped fussing with his soccer bag.

"Ready to go?"

"I don't see why I couldn't get a ride home with Mom."

"Because I want to talk to you." Matthew placed an

arm over Derrick's shoulders as they made their way to his car. He felt Derrick's resentment in the stiff set of his muscles, but his son didn't shake him off.

Matthew waited until they were both in the car before he started. "I guess you're pretty angry at me."

"Oh, yeah? What gave you that idea?"

"You wish I wasn't representing Coach Keller."

There was a pause, then Derrick tore into him. "Why are you? It's sick what he did to Sarah! How could you defend a guy like that?"

Matthew waited a moment for Derrick to catch his breath before responding. "Have you considered that Coach Keller might be innocent?"

"You think Sarah's a liar?"

"No. But cases like this can be more complicated than they appear. When Coach Keller came to talk to me, he was adamant he hadn't done anything wrong."

"Sarah wouldn't lie about something so serious."

"It's hard to see the truth sometimes when you have two people—two people you like—and they're telling you conflicting stories."

"I believe Sarah. Something bad happened to her. You can just tell. She's different."

"I'm sorry about that, son. Our system has to protect children from adults who abuse them. But it also has to protect innocent men from false accusations." Was any of this getting through to Derrick? Matthew couldn't tell. He had crossed his arms over his chest and was staring out the front window.

"You say something bad happened to Sarah and you

may be right. You're probably right. Was it Coach Keller's fault? Every kid on your soccer team, and every one of their parents, has an opinion about that. And, yes, it seems that most of them have decided Coach Keller is guilty."

Gillian certainly had. And she'd imparted her judgment to their son.

"But the thing is, Derrick, it isn't our job to judge. That's why we have a legal system with courts and lawyers."

"But everyone already knows what happened."

"No, they don't. But let's say, for the sake of argument, that Coach Keller is guilty. Do you think it's fair to blame his son for that?"

Matthew let those words sink in, then added, "How did you feel when that guy on your team asked you why I was defending Coach Keller? Do you think it's fair to blame Daniel for something his father may or may not have done?"

"I'm not the only one."

"Maybe you can't control what the other guys say and do. But you can set an example."

"If I was nice to Daniel, they'd think it was because of you. They'd think I was on Coach Keller's side."

"You don't have to be on anybody's side to be fair to Daniel."

"It's not that easy, Dad."

His son was on the verge of tears. Matthew remembered what Gavin had said. Derrick probably already felt bad for how he'd treated Daniel. "No, it isn't easy, son. Doing the right thing often isn't."

He started driving then, but as he signaled for the corner toward his ex-wife's home, Derrick asked him to turn around.

"You know how you said I should apologize? Would you drive me to Daniel's house now so I could do it?"

Yes. His words had sunk in. Matthew could feel his heart expanding with pride in his son. "Of course I will."

CHAPTER TWELVE

DERRICK WAS VISIBLY nervous as they pulled up in front of the Keller residence, but he stepped out onto the street resolutely. Matthew accompanied him up the walkway to the house, where they paused.

"You're doing the right thing." Matthew put a hand on his son's shoulder, then rang the bell.

Leslie Keller opened the door. From the soccer party, Matthew remembered a busy, friendly woman, on the plump side but well groomed, with a pretty sparkle in her eyes. That sparkle was missing now, as was the good grooming and the bustling personality.

"Leslie, how are you doing?" He held out his hand. Hers felt limp, almost rubberlike in his grip. "We met at the soccer party at the beginning of the year, but there were so many people you may not remember me. I'm—"

"Matthew Gray. My husband's attorney. I remember." Her gaze shifted to the boy by his side.

"And this is my son, Derrick."

Her gaze had skimmed over Derrick; now it returned to him sharply. "You're the boy—" She stopped. She had backed up to give them room to enter, but threw a protective glance over her shoulder.

"Derrick would like to speak with Daniel, if that's okay. He's here to apologize," Matthew added, since clearly, Leslie regretted having let them in the house.

She didn't kick them out. But neither did she welcome them. "Wally," she called.

Her husband appeared, and became agitated as soon as he saw who was there. "Has something happened?"

"No," Matthew reassured him. "We're here so my son can apologize to Daniel for some things that have been happening at school and on the soccer field."

Derrick seemed to grow smaller with each passing minute. If he could make himself invisible right now, Matthew had no doubt that was exactly what he would do.

"Hello, Derrick," Wally said. "Daniel's in his room. You can talk to him there." He pointed down the hall to a room with a closed door. After a glance at his father, Derrick headed in that direction.

"I understand my son has been giving Daniel a hard time," Matthew said to the couple once Derrick was out of hearing range. "I'm sorry about that. I know that what you're going through has to be very tough."

"Tough? That's putting it mildly." Wally indicated the sofa in the living room to the left. "Might as well sit while you're waiting."

"Thanks." Matthew chose one of the armchairs, curious to see where the Kellers would sit. The discord between them was pretty obvious. He wondered how deep it went. If charges were laid and Wally couldn't count on his wife's support, it wouldn't bode well for him.

Husband and wife both settled on the sofa, though on opposite ends. Leslie stared at the far wall, her expression resentful. For a few minutes the two men made stilted conversation about the weather and recent road blockages due to construction.

Wally didn't mention the soccer team and Matthew didn't bring it up, either. The Blazers were missing Coach Keller's expertise, but right now that would be cold comfort.

Finally, Leslie snapped under the pressure. "How much longer is this going to go on?"

"I wish I could tell you. On the positive side, the fact that the police haven't laid charges yet means they aren't very confident about their case."

"So they think he's innocent?"

Matthew hated to dash the hope that had sparked in her eyes. "They're still investigating, Leslie, so, no, they haven't concluded that Wally is innocent."

She sank back against the cushions. "How much longer will they keep the case open?"

"It could be weeks."

"Weeks." Her eyes went as dull as they'd been when she'd met him at the door. She stood and left the room. Matthew suspected she was going to cry.

Her husband appeared equally distraught at the news. "I don't know if I can stand this for much longer.

I don't mind so much for me. But watching Leslie suffer… And seeing the changes in the kids…"

He dropped his head into his hands. "Word got out at the office. Now even my job is in jeopardy."

"I'm sorry. This is difficult, Wally, but we still have hope."

He lifted his head. "Do we?"

"No charges have been laid yet," Matthew reminded him.

"Believe me, I'm grateful for that. But even if they never decide to arrest me, what will this do to my future? Will the people of West Hartford forget what I've been accused of? Will the neighbors start talking to my wife again? Will the kids at school stop tormenting my children?"

Matthew felt for the guy, especially since he knew his son had contributed to the Keller family's pain. "I can't answer that."

"This is so bloody unfair. All I wanted to do was coach some kids at soccer."

"You were a great coach."

"So why did this kid tell those lies about me? I was always nice to her. Never got upset when she interrupted our practices."

"Maybe that's why. It's hard to get inside the head of people who've been abused. Sometimes they're so afraid of the truth they make up stories."

"But does this girl know what she's done to me? Done to my family? If I could just talk to her—"

"Forget it. That can't happen."

"But she couldn't tell those lies if we were face-to-face. She couldn't."

"I'm serious, Wally. You can't talk to her."

The sound of boys' voices down the hall interrupted them. When Daniel and Derrick entered the living room, Matthew was glad to see relief in the expressions of both. Some air had been cleared between them, at least.

"Things okay?" he asked his son, and when Derrick nodded, he rose. "Well, I'd better get you home so you can finish up your math homework."

Wally and Daniel walked them out to the car. While the boys talked strategy for their next soccer game, Matthew took the opportunity to give Wally one more warning.

"Hang in there, Wally. I know it's hard to sit back and wait. But right now that's the best you can do."

AFTER HE'D DROPPED OFF his son, Matthew drove despondently toward his apartment. He didn't want to go home, where the only thing waiting was a full bottle of Scotch.

So he decided on Sully's Tavern, instead.

An inspired idea, if he did say so himself. The place was always crawling with lawyers. He'd be sure to find someone he knew, and at least that way he wouldn't be drinking alone.

He parked at home and hailed a cab so he wouldn't compound the errors in judgment he was planning to make tonight. He needed something to drive away the image of Leslie Keller and her sad eyes. He hated cases like this one, absolutely hated them.

If worst came to worst, and Wally Keller was arrested and went to trial, he or Jane would have to cross-examine Sarah Boutin on the witness stand. Probably Jane, since he was supposed to be low-profile on this case.

Jane would hate trying to discredit the testimony of a twelve-year-old girl who had obviously suffered. But that was one of the ugly realities about their jobs.

As the cab slowed to a stop in front of Sully's, Matthew peeled a twenty from his wallet. "Keep the change."

Out on the street, he could swear the air carried the scent of expensive brandy and single-malt Scotch. He hurried down the half flight of stairs, the music inside growing louder with each step.

It was nine-thirty on a Friday night and the place was packed. He made his way to the bar and found a stool. Already he'd spotted a few familiar faces. He nodded at two guys he'd met at a conference on diversity and demographic changes in the legal profession.

The barkeeper raised his eyebrows at him.

"Glenlivet. With water and ice," he added, thinking that would temper the effects of the alcohol a little. He didn't know where this reckless impulse to get drunk had come from, but now that he was here, he was glad.

He glanced back at the two guys, then did a double take. A woman was sitting with them, and if he wasn't mistaken, she'd been at the conference, too. He concentrated until he recalled her name. Cynthia Stevens—

that was it. They'd met during the break and had talked long enough for him to find out that she, too, was newly divorced. She'd been open to the idea of seeing him again, and he'd taken down her contact information, yet for some reason never used it.

Some reason? *Be honest, Matthew. You haven't been able to look at a woman who wasn't Jane since you left your wife.*

But he couldn't have Jane. She'd made that clear this afternoon. He felt like growling at the frustration of it all.

Why was she so determined to keep things platonic between them? Was it really because they worked together? Or was she simply not as attracted to him as he was to her? But the way she'd kissed him...that hadn't felt faked.

The barkeeper served his drink. "Thanks." Matthew picked up the glass, then took a drink. Nice. He glanced around the room again and considered wandering by Cynthia Stevens's table and checking out his reception.

But then another woman caught his attention.

Damn it, was that Jane?

It sure was. And she was sitting with a man. They had a table in the back corner and were leaning toward one another, all cozy and personal.

Hell, if she was seeing someone, she could have done him the courtesy of letting him know. Matthew grabbed his drink, took a longer swallow this time, then headed her way.

As he walked, the craziness of the situation began

to sink in. What would he say to her? He was going in without a plan, which meant he was certain to make a fool of himself and—

Whoa. The guy she was with seemed familiar. Matthew didn't have to think long to figure it out. It was the man Jane had been talking to on the phone this morning. The private investigator. Damn it, he'd *known* the guy was hitting on her.

"Liam James." He recalled the name just as he reached their table. Both Jane and the private investigator started, and turned in his direction.

"Don't tell me you got results back from Maine already," Matthew continued, ignoring Jane's frown.

"Hello, Matthew." Liam rose to shake his hand. He glanced at Jane, probably wanting a cue about how to proceed, but she was gazing stonily at the drink in her hands.

"Care to join us?" Liam asked, falling back on simple courtesy.

Matthew had no doubt that the invitation had been made on the unspoken understanding that this was a private conversation and it would be rude to butt in.

"Sure." He pulled an extra chair to the table. After setting down his glass, he folded his arms with studied ease. "Hi, Jane."

He kept looking at her, waiting for her to answer. Finally, she said tightly, "Matthew."

"So." He turned back to Liam. "I assume you're discussing the Keller case. Did you find anything interesting?"

"Actually, I just put out the call today. I won't get anything back until early next week."

"Oh." Matthew pretended surprise, as if he couldn't imagine another reason that Jane and Liam would be sitting together at a table in Sully's Tavern.

"We just had dinner," Liam said. "I'm trying to convince Jane that she works much too hard, keeps crazy hours and needs to take better care of herself."

"And you think hanging out in a bar is the way she should take better care of herself? Personally, I would have suggested making more use of that executive fitness club she just joined. Every now and then it helps to work up a good sweat. Don't you agree, Liam?"

He was being an asshole, and he knew it, yet Matthew couldn't seem to stop himself. Liam was about his age and had the sort of rugged good looks some women preferred. Not that Matthew normally cared how attractive other men were. But in this case, the information seemed relevant.

"Okayyy…" Liam glanced from Matthew to Jane. "Is something going on here that I haven't been told about?"

Jane put her hand over Liam's. "No—"

But at the same moment Matthew said, "Yes."

This time there was no mistaking the anger in Jane's eyes. "Matt. What is the matter with you?"

"Have I been too obtuse? I'm crazy about you."

"How much have you had to drink?"

He lifted his glass. "This is the first." And he took another long swallow.

Jane shook her head, then apologized to Liam. "He's not usually like this. He's had a rotten week."

"Maybe we should move to another table. Or better yet, another bar."

"That's a good idea."

"I'm sorry. Was I interrupting? You two go ahead. I'd like another drink, anyway." Matthew left his glass on their table the way a dog might leave his mark on a tree, then made his way back to the bar.

By the time he got there, he was practically choking on a mixture of anger and embarrassment. Why the hell had he done that? He'd behaved like some sort of caveman.

But even more important, why the hell had Jane gone out with Liam James? Had she forgotten who she had been kissing that afternoon?

The barkeeper looked at him.

"Another."

"Sure."

A moment later he had it, another Scotch, exactly the way he wanted it. Why couldn't women be so easy?

This drink went down faster, smoother than the other. Good thing he'd thought ahead and traveled by cab. He ordered a third. He was halfway through that when he felt a tap on his shoulder.

"What are you trying to prove, Matthew?"

He put down the glass. The warm feeling he got from a glass of alcohol had nothing on the heat he felt from the touch of Jane's hand and the sound of her voice.

"Why are you doing this? You're not a drinker."

He still hadn't dared to meet her eyes. "Where's James?"

She sighed. "He's gone home. He offered me a lift, but my car is still at work."

"So…what? You feel obliged to make sure your drunk colleague gets home safe?"

"I've never seen you like this. Damn it, Matthew, what's wrong with you tonight?"

He swiveled on the stool so they were face-to-face. "You come here on a date, just hours after I've made love to you and you ask me that?"

Even in the dim light he could see her flush.

"We didn't make love, you know."

"We came close."

"Cut it out, Matt. This is not a unilateral decision on my part. Both of our careers and our reputations are at stake."

"So you just decide not to get involved with me, and you don't. It's that simple for you."

"It's not simple." She closed her eyes, and for a second appeared disarmingly vulnerable. But when she spoke again, her voice was strong. "That's why I went out with Liam. I hoped it might help."

"You hoped going out with Liam would *help*. In what way?"

"Maintain our boundaries."

"So that's why you showed up here with *him*. Dressed like *that*."

"I'm wearing the same clothes I wore to work!"

"Yeah, but you took off your jacket. And undid the top button of your blouse."

"Damn it, Matthew. You're being absolutely impossible. I should just leave you here and let you drink yourself into oblivion."

He'd only had three drinks. He wasn't exactly sloshed. But maybe she was right. Maybe he should work toward that goal. "Bartender?" He raised his empty glass.

Jane made a sound of annoyance.

"Weren't you leaving?"

"I am." She took a few steps, then swiveled back to him. "Just reassure me that you aren't going to be stupid enough to get behind the wheel."

"I'll call a cab." He openly leered at her. "But I would rather accept a ride with you."

Her eyes had never been so cold when she said, "You'll find the cab a lot warmer." And then she left.

CHAPTER THIRTEEN

LIFE HAS A WAY of punishing you when you step out of line. Matthew knew this. That was why, when his phone rang before eight on Saturday morning, he was anticipating bad news.

"Hello?" He hoped the word was legible. His mouth felt as though it were full of cotton and paste.

"Matthew? Sorry to call so early on the weekend, but I didn't know where else to turn."

It was Wally Keller. Matthew rolled over to his side, then sat up. His head felt like a snow globe with all the flakes in motion. He let it rest back on the pillow.

"What's wrong?" The police had asked Wally to come into the station. That was his first guess. But he was wrong.

"Some punks spray-painted my car."

Wally's voice was barely audible over the feedback on the line. He was probably on his cell.

"Covered it in profanity," Wally continued. "Daniel was the first to see it. He was up early to do his paper route."

Matthew swore.

"Yeah, that word was on there." Wally laughed shakily. "God, I can't believe I'm making a joke out of this. Poor Daniel was so torn up. He's home with his mother and sister."

That was what the background noise was, Matthew realized. Wally was delivering the morning paper for his son.

"This happened last night?"

"Must have. The car was fine when I went out to get pizza around seven."

"Both your kids were home all night?"

"Yeah. They haven't had much of a social life lately."

Matthew's stomach churned—from last night's alcohol or from sympathy for the Kellers, he wasn't sure. Or maybe it was shame for the way he'd spoken to Jane…

He pushed those regrets to the back of his mind. Wally deserved his full attention right now.

"Look, I can call a body shop and get your car taken care of."

"It's our only vehicle. How am I supposed to get to work? How is Leslie supposed to buy groceries and drive the kids to their soccer games and piano lessons?"

"You could rent something."

"Right. With all the spare cash I have left over from that retainer I paid your legal firm."

"I'm sorry about that, Wally. But our fees are fair. If you want to call around—"

"I didn't mean to complain. I just feel overwhelmed

sometimes. Some kid decides to tell a bunch of ugly lies about you, and not only is your reputation on the line but your marriage, and your savings—"

He stopped, choked up.

Matthew saw this happen to his clients all the time. He considered it the snowball effect. One bad thing happens and causes a chain reaction of negativity with the potential to derail the most stable of lives. "Wally, you'll get through this."

"I'm a big boy. I know life can deal some rough blows. Like I said, it's my kids I'm most worried about. They were just starting to make friends in their new schools. Now they're outcasts. They don't want to go anywhere or do anything. And then this. Some twerps spray-painting the car. It's like—the last straw."

Some twerps. Suddenly, Matthew felt very cold. He tried sitting up again, this time ignoring the pain and nausea. "Any idea which kids damaged your car?"

"I figure it was some of the boys from the soccer team."

"Why?"

"One of the things they wrote on the car was 'Coach Keller Sucks...' I won't finish. It's obscene. The whole thing is obscene. I moved the car to the garage and covered it with an old tarp."

Matthew heard a *whap* as another newspaper hit someone's sidewalk. He stood up. Headed to the kitchen.

Where had Derrick been last night after he'd dropped him off? He was supposed to be grounded. Could he have sneaked out?

No. Matthew refused to believe that of his son. Especially not so soon after he'd given Daniel his apology. Matthew was positive Derrick had been sincerely sorry.

And yet, peer pressure could be a powerful thing…

"Have you called the police yet?"

"You think I should?"

"Definitely."

"It's just…they don't seem like the good guys anymore."

"I can understand that. But what happened to your car…that was a crime. And it may not feel like it these days, but you do have rights." He poured himself a glass of water. Made himself drink it. The second one went down easier. He was probably dehydrated. Five Scotches in the space of an hour was a lot of alcohol to get out of his system.

If he hadn't been so angry and jealous, he'd have gone home once Jane left. But, no, her words had stung, and so he'd ordered two more drinks before he'd finally had the good sense to call a cab.

Jane. How would she be feeling today? He had to apologize, pronto. He wondered when he'd find the time. She was probably still asleep. At ten he was picking Derrick and Violet up for breakfast. Which gave him a couple of hours…

"Is there something I can do to help?"

"No. That's fine."

Matthew persisted. "I'll phone a body shop. Help you get your car in today."

"The sooner the better, I guess."

"That's right. I'll be over in about an hour. Why don't you contact your insurance company while you're waiting."

Doing something proactive would help, Matthew hoped. At least, a little.

AFTER A QUICK shower, Matthew popped a painkiller for his headache and was at the Kellers' by eight-thirty. As he got out of his car, he noticed a bike, with trailer attached—the kind cyclists used to transport babies and toddlers—on the lawn. Wally had indeed used it to deliver his son's newspapers.

His client was waiting for him on the front steps, screened by an overgrown honeysuckle, so that Matthew didn't notice him until he was almost at the front door. He stopped short.

The other man seemed to have aged five years in the past week. He'd lost weight, too. The cheeks on his once-round face were now hollows. His gray eyes appeared larger and more hopeless.

"Want to see the car?" he asked.

Not really.

Matthew nodded. Wally led him through the side door into the garage, where Matthew helped him remove the tarp.

Whoever was responsible for the obscene graffiti had done a thorough job. The entire body of the car, including the windows, was defaced. The sick feeling returned to Matthew's stomach. His son better not have been involved in this.

He didn't know what he would do if he had been.

"Stupid punks," he said. "Give me the keys, Wally. I'll drive this one. You take mine." He handed him the key to his Audi, as well as a piece of paper with the address and directions to the body shop. "It isn't far away, thankfully."

Wally hesitated, then dropped the Taurus's keys into his hand. "We could wait until dark."

"Let's just get it over with. The sooner we get this into the shop, the sooner you'll have it back."

"Okay." Wally ducked into the house one more time and emerged with a suitcase.

Matthew raised his eyebrows.

"Leslie and I made a few decisions this morning. Daniel was still in his room. Wouldn't talk to her, wouldn't talk to me. It's not fair that I'm putting my family in this situation. I'm going to move out until everything's resolved." He turned his gaze to the distance. "One way or another."

Matthew's sick feeling worsened. He remembered the day he'd left his family's home, suitcase in hand, totally unsure of what his future would hold. "Where will you go?"

"There's a motel near my office. If you could drive me there after we're finished with the body shop, I'd appreciate it."

Matthew shook his head. He didn't like the sound of this. "Your moving out isn't going to look good."

"You mean it will seem that I'm guilty?"

"If your family doesn't believe in you, why should anyone else?"

"It isn't that they don't believe in me. I just want to protect them from this."

"I understand that. But you'll still be hurting your case."

"Then so be it. I'm not putting my wife and kids through another morning like this one."

AFTER HE'D FINISHED helping Wally, Matthew picked up Derrick and Violet and drove them back to his apartment. The one thing he'd asked Allison to do when she'd decorated was to make it as kid friendly as possible. He knew the house where they lived with their mother would always be the place his children thought of as home, but he wanted them to feel comfortable at his apartment, too. He'd even given Derrick a key, telling him he could drop in any time, though so far he'd never shown up except when he had no choice.

Allison understood all about kid friendly, and as a result, his new couch was comfy and nothing was overly fragile, or couldn't be washed if the kids happened to knock over a soft drink. Matthew let them turn on Saturday cartoons, then went to the kitchen to mix pancakes.

Though he'd never learned to cook, he'd managed to master one meal, and that was breakfast. He actually enjoyed whipping together pancakes, sausages and fruit salad now…especially when he had his kids hanging out with him.

After a few minutes, Violet wandered into the kitchen. "Can I help, Daddy?"

"I was hoping you would say that." He set her on a stool, then gave her a carton of eggs to crack open. He didn't worry when she mixed a bit of shell in with the egg. A bit of crunch wouldn't hurt.

"Are Grandma and Uncle Nick coming over?"

He glanced at the clock on the microwave. "Should be here any minute."

Five minutes later his guests were at the security door downstairs and Derrick was buzzing them in. Derrick and Violet went to open the front door, and Matthew waited a minute before joining the group.

When he'd told his mother that he and Gillian were getting a divorce, his mom had worried that she might see less of the children. For that reason, Matthew went out of his way to get them all together as often as possible.

"Hello, sweetheart." His mom, always petite, even more so now that she was older, reached up to squeeze his cheeks. He endured that, then gave her a big hug. Behind their mother, his brother Nick winked cheekily.

"Hey, bro. When do we eat around here?"

"Uncle Nick wants to know if breakfast is almost ready, Violet. What should we tell him?"

"*I'm* making the scrambled eggs."

"Really? That's all I'll going to eat then," his brother said. "Just scrambled eggs for me, Matt."

Violet giggled. "What about coffee, Uncle Nick? You always drink coffee."

Breakfast was a crazy, happy affair. Gavin had

called their mother to tell her about the pregnancy, and she was thrilled. Matthew could feel something inside himself healing with each teasing comment and joyful smile. For a long time after he'd left Gillian, he'd had an unsettled, homeless feeling. Months after he'd rented his first apartment he'd felt that way. But this morning he finally felt some hope. Even his relationship with Derrick seemed to be getting better.

Once everyone had eaten, Violet asked her grandmother to play Trouble with her—her favorite board game. Derrick deigned to play with them, since the alternative was helping out with the dishes.

That left Matthew and Nick alone in the kitchen for a few minutes. Matthew expected his brother to grill him about the sexual abuse case, but Nick was strangely silent.

"What's up?" he finally asked. "You're quiet without the kids around."

"I've got a bit of a problem."

Matthew stopped what he was doing. He couldn't remember the last time Nick had admitted to a problem. "What is it?" he asked, worry making his tone sharp.

"Back off, bro. I've got it covered."

"Hey, I didn't mean to be a jerk. Tell me. Pretend I'm Gavin," he added, only partly joking.

"Well, the thing is, my current girlfriend…"

Who would she be? He didn't dare ask, even though he would have liked a name.

"I thought we had things covered, but something slipped up and now she's pregnant."

"Holy crap." He couldn't believe it. Nick went through girlfriends faster than Matthew changed his Brita water filter. If anyone had safe sex mastered, it was his brother. Then again, the odds eventually had to work against you. "What are you going to do?"

"Have a baby, I guess."

The two brothers looked at each other, then, slowly, Matthew smiled. A moment later, so did Nick.

"Congratulations, bro." He gave him a hug.

"Thanks." Nick seemed taken aback, but pleased.

"Have you told Mom yet?"

Nick's smile vanished. "Hell, no. And don't you, either. Jessica and I want to wait and make the announcement after we're married."

Jessica. Matthew filed the name for future reference. "Wait a minute. You didn't tell me you were getting married."

"That's what you do when you have a baby, isn't it?"

Not necessarily, Matthew thought, but he swallowed his misgivings. "If you love her, then, yes, that's what you do."

"Right." Nick nodded, then started drying dishes again. Matthew noted he hadn't said anything in response to his comment about loving Jessica, but he must or he wouldn't be doing this.

"When do we get to meet her?"

"Soon," Nick said. But he refused to set a date.

JANE OFTEN WENT into work on the weekend, and on Saturday afternoon she chose a route that happened to take her past Matthew's apartment. It was a sophomoric sort of thing to do, and she knew it. But somehow, she couldn't help herself.

She slowed the car as she drove past his building, not really expecting to see him but just…because. Without thinking, she pulled into a vacant parking spot across the street, then let her head sink to the steering wheel for a moment.

She wanted to ring the buzzer and find out if he was home. But she couldn't do that. She just couldn't.

She straightened, then inhaled deeply. She was stopped next to a small park. Three little girls were on the swings, laughing. Jane lowered her window, just to hear the happy sound. In the distance, a man was kicking a soccer ball around with an older boy and a toddler.

An ache of longing was building in the pit of her stomach before she realized who it was. Matthew seemed to spot her at the same time. He shielded his eyes from the sun and stared toward her parked car.

Caught.

She couldn't just drive away now that Matt knew she was here, so she climbed out of the driver's seat, mind scrambling for an excuse for being there.

She headed across the grass, her heels making divots in the soil with every step. Derrick ignored her approach and, taking the soccer ball from his father, began dribbling it in the opposite direction.

"Hi, Matt. I was just on my way to the office…" Her voice trailed off. She still didn't have a reason for stopping by.

"It's nice to see you." His smile was warm. "But I'm sorry. I don't have time to talk business now."

"Because you're playing with me and Derrick, right, Daddy?"

"That's right. Jane, this is my daughter, Violet." He bent to his daughter's level. "Jane is someone I work with. Can you say hi, honey?"

Violet nodded. "Hi." Then she turned to her father. "She's pretty."

Taking a cue from Matthew, Jane crouched in front of the girl and took her hand. "It's nice to meet you, Violet. You have a pretty name."

"It's a flower," the little girl explained. "Daddy, can we go to the swings now? I'm tired of soccer."

Matthew seemed torn. Derrick was about twenty feet away with the soccer ball, and Jane guessed Matthew wanted to go to him.

Speaking to Violet, she said, "Would you like me to push you on the swings while your daddy and Derrick play soccer?"

Violet's eyes brightened, and when he saw her enthusiasm, Matthew accepted the offer with a smile of gratitude. "You're sure you have time?"

"Yes." She held out her hand to the little girl again. Violet's small, warm palm in hers brought out a strong response, one she'd never expected.

Did she like kids?

Yes. She now knew the answer for certain. She liked them very much.

SATURDAY PASSED all too quickly. Playing in the park, having Jane show up and join them, had been the undisputed highlight. Matthew's only regret was that she'd turned down his invitation to join them for dinner afterward. Claiming she still needed to get to the office, she'd left them abruptly. He hadn't had a chance to talk to her privately at all.

He and the kids had gone out for an early dinner of Vietnamese food. Between mouthfuls of lemon chicken and noodles, Violet chatted about Jane. She was clearly taken by her, but Derrick just concentrated on his food until Matthew changed the subject.

Not until later, after Violet had been dropped off at home with her mother and he and Derrick were alone in the apartment, did Matthew have a chance to tell his son about what had happened to the Kellers' car.

"Coach Keller is worried some of the guys from the soccer team did it," he concluded.

He and Derrick were on the sofa. A mindless sitcom was playing on the TV, but he'd hit the mute button before bringing up the subject.

Earlier he'd decided that Derrick deserved the same treatment he afforded his clients—innocent until proven guilty. Especially since making his peace with Daniel Keller. Matthew just didn't believe his son could have spray-painted those awful words on the Kellers' car that very same night.

Derrick turned to him. "You don't think I did it, do you?"

"No."

Derrick's face reddened and tears filled his eyes. Matthew was deeply touched to see how much his faith meant to his son. He put his arm around Derrick's shoulders and gave him a hug.

"I was really proud of you the other night. Apologizing after you've hurt someone is one of the hardest things a man has to do."

He thought of Jane, and his own outstanding apology. He'd had the urge to talk to her in the park about it, but she deserved more than a few hurried minutes between activities with his children.

"Well, I imagine the police will find out who defaced Coach Keller's car. I'm just sorry that Daniel and his sister are being put through this."

"I'm sorry, too." A second passed. "What will happen to the guys who did it, Dad?"

"That depends." Matthew twisted for a view of his son's face. "Do you think it's possible some of the boys from the team did it?"

"I don't know," Derrick mumbled.

"If you do, you should say something, son."

"I said I don't know."

It wasn't an entirely satisfactory answer. But Matthew decided to leave it at that.

CHAPTER FOURTEEN

JANE WAS NOT LOOKING forward to the partners meeting on Monday morning. Partly because she didn't want to face off with Eve. But mostly because she was afraid she couldn't handle being in the same room as Matthew.

This weekend he'd run her through a gamut of emotions the likes of which she'd never experienced.

On Friday night he'd made her steaming mad at the bar—but he'd also made her hot in other ways. Matthew, all jealous and primal and verging on out-of-control, had awakened her own deep and dark desires. He'd made her angry and frustrated and almost crazy with her need for him.

Then, on Saturday afternoon, he'd melted her heart. Watching him with his kids and getting to spend a little time on her own with Violet had given Jane a taste of what life with Matthew would have to offer. And it was everything she'd thought she'd never have.

But she couldn't let herself dwell on that. *Focus on work,* she ordered herself. *Focus on the Keller case.*

Things were not going well on that score, either.

When she'd made it to work on Saturday, she'd found an e-mail from Leslie Keller, and was not impressed that Matthew hadn't told her that the Kellers' car had been vandalized or that their client had moved out of the family home.

That was *not* a good development. She should have been consulted. Who was the head lawyer on this case, anyway?

Jane tossed her briefcase onto her desk, scattering the papers she'd stacked so neatly when she'd left late on Saturday. She had fifteen minutes before the partners meeting. Might as well check for new e-mail messages.

Finally, she couldn't put off any longer heading to the meeting. She gathered her notebook and pen, then took a moment to straighten her jacket.

A memory flashed. Matt saying: *"So that's why you came here with him. Dressed like that."*

Had he really found her sexy just because she'd removed her jacket and undone one button of her blouse? She wondered what he would have said if she'd unfastened *two* buttons. Enough so he could glimpse the lacy red bra she'd been wearing that day.

How crazy would he have gotten then? she wondered. Crazy enough to put his arms around her and press his body as close as he had when they were in her living—

"Jane?"

Crap. She started, dropping her notebook, then felt her face flush as the very man she'd been thinking about—no, be honest, *fantasizing* about—entered her office.

Matthew was wearing a dark gray suit, a white shirt with gray stripes and a charcoal tie with various shades of gray and white stripes. The look was very professional, very sharp…and very sexy.

"Sorry for barging in." He retrieved her notebook and her pen, giving her a chance to admire his thick, dark hair. His fingers managed to touch hers as he passed her the items, and she felt a zap of forbidden pleasure.

"I wanted to apologize before the meeting," he continued.

He was standing too near. Either that, or the room had suddenly warmed up a couple of degrees.

She reminded herself how angry she'd been on Friday. "I guess I won't have to worry about Liam inviting me out for dinner again."

"Well, good. At least I solved that problem for you."

"Matthew…"

"Sorry." He held up his hands in a conciliatory gesture. "Honestly, I really am sorry. I had no right to interrupt your date. No right to talk to you the way I did."

"No, you didn't." And yet, she'd liked it. What would he say if she told him that? Her cover would be blown. He would finally realize how totally and absolutely besotted she was with him.

"Okay, so we've agreed that I'm a jerk and you'll never date again. Now, let's go to that meeting."

He made her feel like laughing. But she wouldn't. She fell into step beside him as he headed for the main conference room.

"So how plastered did you end up getting on Friday?"

"You don't want to know. Let's just say that when my phone rang the next morning, I had an inkling of what brain surgery would feel like without the anesthesia. Hi, Tracey," he added, as they passed a legal assistant with her arms full of files.

"Hi, Matthew." The young woman smiled brightly, tossing back her red hair in a decidedly flirtatious manner.

A second later, Jane whispered, "Did you notice the way she smiled at you?" In a louder tone she said, "That phone call wouldn't have been from Wally Keller, would it?"

Matthew raised his eyebrows. "Heard about that, did you?"

"Why didn't you call me?"

"I needed to focus on my kids this weekend. Thanks for taking Violet to the swings, by the way. She had a lot of fun. Couldn't stop talking about it."

Jane felt her cheeks grow warm. Did that mean Violet had liked her? "It was my pleasure."

"Anyway, back to why I didn't tell you about Keller. I had an apology to deliver before I talked to you about anything else, and no time or privacy to deliver it."

She supposed she could forgive him for that. "Well, I'm not happy about his moving out of the family home."

"Me, either."

"It'll appear as if his wife thinks he's guilty."

"Don't I know it."

They were at the conference-room doors now, and Matthew paused, waiting for her to enter first. Davis Norton and several junior partners were already in the room. Jane nodded in response to their greetings, then took the same chair she'd occupied the previous week. Matthew settled next to her.

Silently she beseeched him to be cautious.

"What?" he asked sotto voce. "We're working on the same case. It makes sense to sit beside each other."

Jane settled her notebook on the table. Davis Norton was presiding over the coffee as usual. He offered her a cup, then Matthew. She'd just enjoyed her first sip when Eve walked into the room, along with Russell.

Conversation hushed now that all three senior partners were present. Eve, head held regally high, gazed directly from Jane to Matthew, then back to Jane. Her eyebrows rose slightly and she tilted her head just a fraction to the left.

It was the most subtle of messages, but Jane received it all too clearly.

Eve had noted—and disapproved of—the fact that Jane and Matthew were sitting next to each other.

Jane scribbled the date angrily into her notebook. What the hell was this? Junior high school? It shouldn't matter where she sat. Where anyone sat.

And yet, she knew it did matter. Matthew sitting beside her was a subtle signal that their relationship had changed. Some might take it to mean they were now comfortable working together. Eve obviously felt it meant quite a bit more than that.

But where others sat in the meeting was important, too, and as Eve and Russell seated themselves at opposite ends of the oval table, Jane exchanged a surprised look with her fellow junior partners. When she glanced at Matthew, she could see that he, too, was puzzled.

In the past Russell and Davis, as the two most senior partners, occupied the symbolically important seats at the head and foot of the table. Why was Eve now sitting in Davis's place?

Jane waited for Russell to explain what was going on, but he chaired the meeting in the same manner as always, beginning with a review of current cases, then moving on to introducing and assigning new cases.

This week she ended up with several petty misdemeanors and a juvie case. None was out of the ordinary.

Matthew let her lead the discussion of the Keller case, and she provided a brief overview of the week's progress—which wasn't much since charges still hadn't been laid against their client.

The meeting was all but over when Davis suddenly took the floor.

"Some of you may be wondering why I'm not occupying my usual place at the table. It is with both great anticipation and a significant amount of sorrow that I announce my intention to resign from the firm effective the end of this month."

Though an announcement like this had been anticipated for years, several junior partners gasped at the news.

"Most of you know that our daughter recently moved to Australia to marry a fellow she met when she was hiking through Europe. Well, Christy is pregnant, and her mother and I have decided we're going to move to Adelaide as soon as the baby is born.

"Obviously, the commute from Australia to the office is a little more than I can handle at sixty-nine. Maybe when I was younger…"

Everyone chuckled, but beneath the humor, Jane knew, was a lot of speculation. What would this change mean for the rest of them? Russell didn't leave them wondering long.

He announced plans for a retirement party, then tacked on the news everyone was waiting to hear. "As you know, since its inception this firm has been run by a triumvirate of senior partners. With Davis's retirement, we will be seeking a new senior partner at Brandstrom and Norton, and every junior partner in this room is a possible candidate for that position."

The next gasp was subdued but loaded with portent.

As junior partners, they all shared in firm profits, but as senior partners, their financial stake would be higher, plus they would have a say in strategic management decisions. Making senior partner was one of the capping achievements of a legal career, on par with a judicial appointment.

Jane glanced around the table. Not one person sitting here wouldn't kill to be the chosen one. Her included.

"We'll be making our final decision at the end of the

month," Russell told them. "Right after the retirement party." With that he adjourned the meeting, and everyone stood up to leave.

As she gathered her papers, Jane had the feeling of being watched. She lifted her head to find Eve's large, dark eyes fixed on her again.

Matthew, too, noticed the look. He bent close so only Jane could hear. "What's Eve staring at you for?"

"Do you really have to ask?" Grimly, Jane filed out of the room and returned to her office. The smallest misstep now would put any of the junior partners out of the running for the promotion. If she and Matthew suddenly became romantically involved, they could both kiss their chances for senior partner goodbye.

JANE WAS CLEARLY UPSET after the partners meeting and Matthew wanted to talk to her, but he was forestalled by Russell.

"Have you got a minute?" the senior partner asked him. Matthew didn't dare say no. Russell led the way to his corner office. It was a large, beautifully appointed room, showcasing yet more of the New England art that the senior partners at Brandstrom and Norton were so fond of.

Matthew knew little about art. He'd been happy to leave the selection of the canvases in his apartment to Allison. He sat down in view of an abstract piece that in the past he'd found made his head hurt if he studied it too long.

He brought his gaze back to the man who wanted

to speak with him. "That was an interesting announcement at today's meeting. I'm going to miss Davis. The place won't be the same without him."

"Davis is an excellent lawyer and a true gentleman," Russell agreed, tugging on his trousers above his knee to create a little slack, then crossing one leg over the other. It was an effeminate posture, but Russell had the confidence and stature to carry it off without losing one iota of his masculine authority.

"But Davis hasn't been actively practicing for several years now," Russell continued. "It's time we found a replacement for him in the firm. And you, Matthew..."

Matthew waited.

"You are definitely one of the top contenders for the position."

He felt a rush of pride and excitement, quickly followed by concern for Jane. She was just as qualified. He wanted the senior partnership. Badly. But not at her expense.

"There are others who have earned this just as much as I have."

"How chivalrous of you to point that out. I trust you're thinking of Jane?"

"Among others. But, yes, Jane would be one of the more qualified of the junior partners, I would think."

"You're right. Jane is ambitious, smart and hardworking. Are you up for the competition?"

Matthew didn't know how to answer that. Frankly, he didn't like the idea of competing against Jane. On the other hand, he wasn't going to bow out of the race.

"If you're asking whether I'd like to be considered for the position, then damn right I would."

Russell laughed. "That's what I thought. I knew Eve was wrong when she said something was going on between the two of you."

MATTHEW WAS AT HIS DESK, trying to decide whether to tell Jane about his unsettling conversation with Russell, when his phone rang. It was Wally Keller, and he was extremely agitated. At first he spoke so quickly Matthew couldn't understand a word.

"Take a deep breath, Wally." He grabbed his pen so he'd be ready to make notes. "Okay. Now talk. Slowly."

"The police just called me. They want me to come to the downtown station tomorrow at ten. Does this mean they're going to arrest me?"

Yeah, probably it did. Matthew felt terrible for the poor man. If Wally had found the past week difficult to bear, the next little while would be even harder.

"If they do charge you, make sure you don't say anything. Tell them you want your lawyer present."

"So you'll come with me?"

"I could. But at this point it isn't necessary. I'll be with you the next day, when we go to see the judge."

"The next day… Are you saying I'll spend the night in jail?"

"Just the one night, until the arraignment, where bail will be set." He paused to let that sink in. "There will be conditions to your arraignment, Wally, including the most obvious one—that you should continue to avoid all contact with the Boutins and other members of the soccer team."

He expected Wally to say something to that, and when he didn't, Matthew became suspicious. "Wally? Is something else wrong?"

"I, um, I did something kind of stupid yesterday."

Damn. Damn. Damn. Matthew scrawled a big black X over the piece of paper on his desk. "You tried to talk to Sarah Boutin."

"I just wanted her to understand what she was doing to me. I was sure she would admit that she was lying if she realized how much her allegations were hurting my kids and my wife."

Matt swore. "Am I not charging you enough, Wally?"

"Huh?"

"Maybe if you had to pay more for my advice, you'd actually take it."

"I'm sorry. I should have listened." Wally sounded utterly exhausted and discouraged. Matthew didn't have the heart to berate him any further.

"Tell me exactly what happened."

"I drove by the Boutins' place around dinnertime on Sunday. I was depressed because I knew my own family would be sitting at the dining-room table without me. I went round the back of the house and Sarah happened to be out there, high up in a big tree in the backyard."

"Was she alone?"

"Yeah."

A twelve-year-old girl sitting by herself in a tree? That struck Matthew as strange, and he scrawled a note of it. "Go on."

"I made some noise so I wouldn't startle her. Then, when she turned in my direction, I said her name. The next thing she was screaming her head off. I tried to tell her I only wanted to talk to her. That I would never, ever hurt her or even touch her. But she kept screaming, and eventually, her mother showed up."

"How long did that take? Until the mother came out."

"Quite a long time. I think she must have been in the bath because she was wearing a robe."

Taking a bath at dinnertime on a Sunday seemed a little odd, also. Matthew made another note. "Where was Sarah's brother?"

"I'm not sure. I got the impression Robert wasn't home. Maybe he was at a friend's house."

"Okay. So what happened next?"

"Claudia Boutin called her daughter to come inside, and told me she was phoning the cops."

"And did she?"

"I guess she must have, but I didn't stay around to find out. I drove back to the motel. Didn't talk to anyone else until this morning, when I showed up at work."

"Is that where the cops called you?"

"Yes."

"Okay." Matthew sighed. "There's not much we can do at this point, Wally. You'll have to go to that appointment tomorrow." He outlined in more detail what Keller could expect.

Getting arrested was an unsettling experience for the average citizen. Unfortunately, nothing Matthew might do could make it easier for Wally. Matt's time was best spent preparing for the arraignment the next day. "Both Jane and I will be there," he assured him.

After ending the call, he stared at his notes. So it had come to this. Hell. He wondered how Leslie Keller would handle the news.

CHAPTER FIFTEEN

JANE WAS ON THE PHONE when Matthew walked into her office. He sprawled in one of the chairs meant for clients and managed to appear as comfortable as if he was at home on his sofa. She resented that he could be so relaxed when just being in the same room with him put her on edge.

She rotated her desk chair so that her back was to him. "I appreciate it. That was very fast work."

"Who are you talking to?" Matthew asked.

She ignored him, trying to focus on her conversation.

"Is this anything to do with the Keller case? Because we could use a break about now."

Still ignoring him, she said, "Yes, I think so, too. But I'm kind of busy now." She resisted the urge to rub her eyes. She *was* tired. It hadn't been a good weekend for sleep.

Too much dreaming about Matthew and the way he'd made her feel at the bar on Friday. She'd tried to burn off the sexual energy at the gym, but her only reward had been sore muscles.

"Okay. You bet. See you soon, Liam." She spun her chair around, then hung up the phone.

"Liam?" Matthew stood again and moved closer to her desk, making use of every inch of his height. "Didn't I take care of that guy the other night?"

"Stop towering over me like that. And stop talking about Liam as if he was my boyfriend. Have you forgotten he's one of the best investigators we have at our disposal?"

"Dispose is exactly what I'd like to do with him."

Matt was doing the jealous thing again. Why did she like it so much? She was supposed to be a modern, enlightened woman. She *was* a modern, enlightened woman.

"Liam got a report back from his guy in Maine."

"I hope it's good news, since I just heard from Wally, and the police have asked him to come to the station tomorrow at ten."

They exchanged glances heavy with the shared understanding of what this meant.

"Poor Wally," she said.

"I'm guessing Liam James didn't call with good news."

"I'm afraid not."

SINCE THEY BOTH HAD TO GO to court that morning, they decided to talk while they walked. The streets of Hartford were quiet on this pleasant May morning. They turned onto Washington Street, retracing a route they'd traveled many times.

"I can't believe Wally was that stupid. Why do our clients do these stupid, stupid things?"

Jane was ranting because he'd just told her about Wally's attempt to speak to Sarah Boutin. Matt understood her frustration. Hadn't he told him that the worst thing he could do was to speak to the victim? And what had their client done?

Matthew shook his head. "It's exasperating, but it happened. Now we have to deal with the fallout."

"Have you talked to his wife?"

"Not yet. I intend to call her later this afternoon."

"Leslie's probably freaking out about the arrest."

"If she even knows. He may not have told her." Matthew put a hand on Jane's elbow as the pedestrian light in front of them turned red.

"We could have made that," Jane objected, glancing at her watch.

"Let's get there in one piece," he suggested. "Hopefully, with no bloodstains. So what did Liam have to report? Or was he just phoning to ask for a date?"

"A date? No worries about that. You've left him with the mistaken impression that you are romantically interested in me."

Matt tightened his hold on her arm. "Mistaken?"

They stared into each other's eyes for a moment, then she pulled away. "Light's green."

She took off so fast he had to hurry to catch up to her again. "Okay, so if he wasn't calling for a date, why did he call?"

"It isn't good, Matt. The reason the Kellers left

Maine was to give their marriage a fresh start. Wally had an affair."

Matthew swore. "You're kidding me."

"It gets worse. The woman he had the affair with was his children's babysitter. And she was twelve years his junior."

MATTHEW HAD TO ADMIT that he'd taken Coach Keller's case for the worst reason possible—because he'd thought the man was innocent. Defense attorneys didn't work that way. They didn't *think* that way. Judges were the ones who worried about guilt and innocence. For attorneys it was all about advocacy. A client came to you and you went to bat for him. No matter if he'd committed the crime or not.

Defense attorneys were just one piece in the justice puzzle, and when they started viewing themselves as an innocent man's crusader, then they weren't doing their job. They were simply lawyers gone amok.

That was what had almost happened to him. So in a way, he *deserved* all these crappy developments.

Matthew signaled for another Scotch. The bar was full and loud, and it smelled too much of alcohol and expensive cologne. Lawyers were packed in all around him, men and women of the bar eager to put the day behind them.

He glanced at the entrance. Craned his neck trying to get a clear view. No sign of Jane yet. They'd agreed to get together after court to discuss strategy. They'd decided against meeting at the office, where Jane felt their every move was being watched by Eve and the others.

She'd also objected to meeting at either of their homes.

Which had left Sully's.

If he became an alcoholic, it would be all Jane's fault, he thought, as he lifted his glass to his lips for a satisfying swallow. As the alcohol burned in his empty stomach, he decided it would be smart to order some food. He asked for loaded nachos, and a few minutes later a huge plate of corn chips smothered in melted cheese, peppers and diced tomatoes was set in front of him.

"Sorry I'm late."

He caught a whiff of Jane's perfume as she slid onto the bar stool next to his. His body responded at the sight and smell of her. Needing to touch her, he brushed his fingers over her hand on the pretext of taking her brief-case and setting it on the floor next to his.

"Mmm. Nachos." Jane ordered a glass of wine, then helped herself to the corn chips as she and Matt exchanged stories about the day. He finished his Scotch. Switched to ice water.

Jane raised an eyebrow. "Practicing moderation?"

"In some things." He gave her an openly admiring look. "You're beautiful. You do know that, right? Even with sour cream on your lips."

She licked off the cream, then shook her head exasperatedly. "You're crazy."

"Because I find you beautiful? Or because I said it?"

The phone tucked in his jacket pocket began to vibrate. He ignored the call, waiting for her response.

"Both." Jane ate some more nachos, then drank a little wine.

He knew his compliment had been summarily dismissed, and that intrigued him. Jane *was* beautiful, though she seemed impervious to the fact. His ex-wife had enjoyed a bit of harmless flirting with other men, smiling and tossing her hair when she elicited an admiring glance from a handsome stranger.

But Jane never seemed to even notice when a guy gave her the once-over.

Her lack of interest in feminine wiles was one of the endearing things about her.

"Did you get a chance to call Leslie Keller?" Jane asked.

"I tried, but there was no answer. So I phoned Wally. Apparently, he did tell his wife about the impending arrest, and her response was to pull the kids out of school, throw them in the car and drive to Florida to stay with her parents." He shoveled more chips into his mouth. As if this junky bar food was going to make him feel better.

Jane's distress was obvious. "Why on earth would she do that?"

"Wally said she doesn't want the kids to know that their father is getting arrested."

"Damn." She shook her head. "His family taking off like that. This is looking worse and worse for Wally."

"I know. On the one hand you can't blame parents

for wanting to protect their kids. But if Leslie believed he was innocent, wouldn't she want the kids to stay and see their father vindicated?"

"She's probably jaded by what happened in Maine."

"Yeah. Tell me more about that. What was the age difference again?"

"Twelve years."

Wally Keller was thirty-four. "So the babysitter was twenty-two. At least she was an adult."

"Only just. She was a college girl, living at home, babysitting to make extra money for tuition."

Jane was right. A thirty-four-year-old man with a young girl of twenty-two. It felt unsavory no matter how you spun it. "How long did the affair last?"

"I'm not sure. We'll have to talk to Wally. At the same time we'd better find out if he has any other sexual indiscretions in his past."

Matthew nodded. "After tomorrow, here's hoping he'll be scared enough to finally tell us the truth."

Jane inclined her head toward him, her eyes narrowed. "You're ticked off. You believed he was innocent. And now you're not sure."

"Stupid of me, I know." The thing was, he'd *wanted* to believe the coach was innocent. Wally had gone out of his way to help Derrick, as well as a bunch of the other boys on the soccer team. Matthew had felt he owed him a favor in return. But that was the way these guys operated, earning the trust of the kids and the parents, positioning themselves to get what they were really after.

It made Matthew sick. It really did. Especially when he thought about the kids who'd been hurt the most. Sarah, of course. But also Wally's children, Daniel and Emily. Even Matthew's own.

"You think you're immune to this stuff," he said, "and then you take on a new case…like this one…and you find you aren't."

Jane covered his hand with hers. "You could still drop out. I'd understand."

Her eyes, usually so cool and analytical, were warm and full of sympathy. Those eyes could be his undoing. And so could her touch.

"Not an option. Neither is staying in this bar. If I don't go now, I won't be able to resist ordering another Scotch. And if I order one more Scotch, I'll end up getting drunk again."

"That doesn't sound like you."

"It isn't. Not normally. The trouble is, this hasn't been a normal week." He put enough money on the counter to cover their tab, then stood up. "Are you coming or staying?"

She hesitated, then ate the last corn chip. "Coming."

JANE KNEW MATTHEW WAS under a lot of stress. She sensed he still wanted to talk, yet she couldn't risk being alone with him. Still, he was striding along the sidewalk as if he knew exactly where he was going, and she was swept with him.

"We still haven't discussed the partners meeting. So what did you think?" he asked.

"I haven't had a chance to process." They crossed the street, then Matthew hailed a taxi. He opened the door and stood back for her to enter.

"Where are we going?"

"Your place."

"Are you kidding?"

"Okay, then. My place."

"Matthew…"

"We can't stand on the street and talk. And I don't feel like a restaurant after those nachos. Can you come up with another option?"

"Fine. Your place." As Matthew gave the driver his address, she slid into the backseat of the taxi and tucked her skirt around her legs.

Matthew followed, sitting close enough that she could feel his broad shoulder pressing against her. His leg was only inches from hers and she imagined him putting a hand on her thigh. Matthew had strong, masculine hands, but she knew his touch would be gentle as he trailed his fingers along the silky fabric of her nylons….

"Thank you, Jane. I really couldn't face being on my own right now."

"No problem." She turned away from him, afraid that her eyes would betray her feelings.

Why was she playing with fire like this, going to his home, when she knew how dangerously attracted to him she was?

At the same time, she cared about him too much to reject him when he needed to talk.

At his place, Matt put on a pot of coffee and invited her to choose some music. She selected a Bach violin concerto to play softly in the background.

"That's very…cerebral," he said. He'd finished with the coffee and was already relaxing on the sofa with his jacket off and tie loosened.

"That's the idea." She sipped the coffee he'd brought out for her, then sat in a comfy armchair a safe distance away. "What did *you* make of Davis's announcement this morning?"

"He hasn't accepted a new client in ages. Plus, he is seventy this year. I can't say I was too surprised."

"The timing is interesting, though. Did you notice how pleased Eve seemed?"

"I did see the way she looked at you," Matthew admitted. "It was a sort of 'cat's swallowed the canary' look."

"She knew that announcement would make you and me competitors."

"It made all the junior partners competitors."

"Yes."

He must have heard the "but" in her voice. "You suspect Eve planned the competition to keep you and me from getting romantically involved?"

"It sounds ridiculous when you say it. Yet she did corner me last week to warn me against getting too close to you."

And now Davis was retiring, and she and Matt were both contenders to be his replacement. Eve couldn't have had any control over the timing of Davis's retirement, yet she'd been so damn pleased about it at the meeting today.

"You know what really gets me about this? Eve is my mentor, dare I say friend? She hired me. And I know she was the one who pushed to have me promoted to junior partner."

"And you feel she's turning on you now?"

"A bit," Jane confessed.

"Eve makes no secret that she chose to focus on her career rather than get married and have a family. Maybe she can't stand to see you having what she couldn't."

"But I don't." In fact, she had made the very same choice as Eve.

"Right now you don't. But maybe that's about to change." Matthew caught her gaze and held it.

They both stopped talking. Jane thought about the feel of Violet's hand in hers. The trusting light in the little girl's eyes when she'd placed her in the swing.

Matthew Gray was a package deal that came with an adolescent son and a toddler daughter. The children might scare away some potential lovers.

For her, they did the very opposite.

The Bach concerto overwhelmed the room as the violin crescendoed in a musical climax. Then the character of the piece abruptly shifted, became slower and subdued.

She stared at her hands. "It isn't about to change."

"Why are you fighting me so hard? Jane, sit beside me. I can't talk to you when you're so far away."

She shook her head. "I can't."

"Why not? If you're not interested in me in a romantic sense, just come here and tell me so." He patted the cushion next to his. Did he realize what he was doing? She thought so. He knew she wasn't immune, that she felt the attraction between them just as much as he did.

She didn't have the nerve to get out of her chair.

"If you're worried about work, don't be. Naturally, the firm isn't going to encourage romantic affairs between partners. But, as I've said, we're both free agents. If we want to be together, no one at Brandstrom and Norton is going to stop us. No one has the right."

"But the promotion…"

"Jane, do you care that much? If you do, we can keep our relationship secret until the announcement is made."

"You're talking about us as if there's a relationship to protect."

"Jane," he said, sounding annoyed. He started to rise from the sofa, then swore when he spilled some of his coffee on his lap.

She hurried to the kitchen, where she grabbed a towel. "Use this." As she tried to pass it to him, though, he grasped hold of her hand, not the towel.

"Do it for me," he said softly.

She shook her head. "Nice try."

But he didn't let her go. "Tell me you're not interested, Jane. Tell me you don't want me to kiss you."

She raised her chin. She could say those things.

Why not? In the courtroom she'd done her fair share of acting. Such as pretending to be surprised when a witness said something she'd coached him to say.

But Matthew would know she was lying.

"I'm a smart person, Matt. I like to make choices that are going to improve my life, not make it harder. And kissing you…that would definitely make my life harder."

CHAPTER SIXTEEN

"INTERESTING CHOICE of word," Matthew said dryly. He blotted the coffee from his pants without letting go of Jane's hand. He'd reached the point where he couldn't talk anymore. Nor could he deny what he felt and what he wanted. When his pants were dry, he sat again, then pulled her onto his lap so she could feel what was happening with his body.

"This is what just *thinking* about kissing you does to me."

Her eyes widened as she felt his arousal. Here was the moment of truth. Matthew didn't know whether to expect a slap on the face or a verbal assault. But Jane just smiled. "Your problem. Not mine."

"I wonder if that's true." He eyed her speculatively, then put a finger on the top button of her blouse.

"Matthew?"

Her breath sounded heavy. He undid the button.

"What are you up to?"

She still wasn't slapping him. That was good. "You did this for Liam."

"I didn't *do it* for anyone. I did it for comfort."

"Liar. You knew it would make you look sexy."

"Wrong. *This* makes me look sexy." With her gaze locked on his, she undid the next button on her blouse.

He caught a glimpse of her curves. And something else. "You're wearing red lingerie." He groaned, then cupped her face with both his hands and kissed her.

Jane melted right into him, and soon the kiss was more than just that. They fell into the sofa, her body on his, so that he could feel all her curves, the warm softness of her, the perfumed silk of her hair against his neck.

Her blouse came untucked, or maybe he had pulled it out from her skirt. He slid his hands up her lean back, stopping at the lacy strap of her bra long enough to loosen the hooks.

She sat up. "Matt…"

He caught his breath. She didn't want him to stop now, did she?

"This isn't smart."

Hell. "Maybe not. But doesn't it feel right anyway?" It did. She belonged in his arms, and every cell in his body knew it.

"It does feel…good."

"Your body is telling you something." He lifted her gently and set her on the sofa so that he could lean over her. With her hair splayed on the cushions, her lips pink and swollen, she was absolutely irresistible. He trailed his fingers down the column of her throat, past her clavicle, to the swell of her breast.

"Listen to your body, Jane." He brushed her nipple

with his thumb, then pushed her bra aside and kissed her there. Her body arched and he slipped his free hand under her back.

"Matt, this feels *too* good. I don't think I want it to stop."

"You don't know how glad I am to hear you say that." He kissed her mouth again, and she curled her body into him. Her skirt was riding up, giving him access to her legs. He slid his hand along her stockings, up her thigh and over the generous curves of her butt. He slipped a finger under her waistband.

"Your panties." He stopped kissing to whisper in her ear. "Are they red, too?"

She smiled, touched his lips with her finger. "Take me to the bedroom and I'll show you."

MATTHEW WAS RESTING on the pillow next to hers. His eyes were closed, but he wasn't sleeping—Jane could tell. "What are you thinking about?"

She couldn't help feeling anxious. It had been a long time since she'd made love, and she wasn't sure if what had just happened—which had seemed wonderful to her—had seemed equally wonderful to Matt.

Sex and the City was a fun show, but it put a lot of pressure on a single woman.

"I'm committing to memory what just happened between us. I don't want to ever forget a second of it."

"So that means...you liked it?"

"Jane." He laughed lightly, then opened his eyes. "You're kidding, right? The first time between new lovers almost never feels this good. Usually, it's a little…well, awkward."

"I didn't feel that way." Which was the truth. She'd felt bold at times, never awkward.

"It showed." He had one of his arms resting at her waist. Now he held her closer, until her nose was right against his chin.

"I take it you liked my red underwear."

She'd only meant to tease him, but she felt the muscles in his arm and chest stiffen.

"If you'd been wearing granny panties and a sports bra, I would have been just as crazy about you. Jane, the sex we just had was great, but you know this thing between us is a lot more than that."

"Yes." She sighed, feeling contented almost despite herself. Maybe a relationship between them could work.

"Jane, answer me something. Why did you tell me not to worry about birth control?"

"You said you were clean." She shifted her head so she could see him. He wasn't the type to sleep around. Was he?

"I am. There's been no one since Gillian."

"Well, so am I. Clean, I mean." She let herself relax again. "So there's nothing to worry about."

"But shouldn't we be worried about pregnancy? Or are you on the pill?"

"I'm not." She'd walked right into this one. But maybe it was for the best. He had to be told, sooner or later. "I'm sterile, Matthew. I can't have children."

JANE'S MATTER-OF-FACT announcement left him stunned for a moment. She couldn't have children. How did she know that? She'd never been married, so presumably she'd never tried.

"Are you sure?"

"Oh, yes."

"Really." He felt blown away by this. Though he'd never dared to actually map out a future with Jane, he realized that on some level he had thought about it. He'd assumed she'd want children. After all, she wasn't yet forty, and he himself had been prepared for more children.

In fact, he'd been looking forward to them.

The sudden realization that there wouldn't be any, that there *couldn't* be any, filled him with sorrow. For him, but especially for Jane.

"What's wrong, Matt? You already have two kids. You should be glad to have those years of diapers and sleepless nights behind you."

She sounded brittle, and he realized he wasn't reacting the way she had hoped. She'd made the announcement so lightly, slipping it into their conversation as if it was no big deal at all.

Was that how she wanted him to respond? As though it didn't really matter?

But of course it did, and he had so many questions. Why was she sterile? Had something happened to her, or had she been born that way? Was this the real reason she'd stayed single for so many years and focused all her energy on her career?

"You still haven't answered my question."

He stared at her numbly. He wanted so badly to say the right thing here.

"Jane, I'm just so—" A noise interrupted him. He realized the front door was opening.

Jane heard it, too. She rose to her elbows. "Do you have a cleaning lady?"

"Yes, but—" The cleaning team had been in just a few days ago. He had a terrible premonition about who this would be.

Something dropped to the floor, then they heard footsteps. "Dad?" It was Derrick. A moment later he was standing at the open bedroom door.

JANE YANKED THE SHEET UP to her chin, mortified, absolutely mortified, that Matthew's son was seeing her this way. "Matthew. Handle this."

She'd never been so angry in her life. How could he have brought her here and made love with her, knowing that his son could walk in at any moment and discover them together?

What if Derrick had arrived half an hour earlier? That would have been even more terrible.

And this was plenty terrible as it was.

"Hang on, son. Give me a minute and we'll talk about this."

But Derrick had already fled from the scene. Five seconds later they heard the front door slam shut.

Matthew swore as he hurried out of bed. He pulled

on his pants, then searched for his socks. Jane got out of bed, too. "What are you going to do?"

"I don't know." Matthew handed her the red panties.

They didn't look so sexy now, Jane thought. In fact, they made her feel ill. She put them on anyway. What choice did she have? She buttoned up her blouse without the bra, then her skirt. Her panty hose were in a puddle on the floor.

"What are you going to tell him?"

"I don't know." Matthew was fastening the buttons on his cuffs. He was calm, cool. Too cool, in her opinion.

"I don't suppose you'd like to tell me how you let this happen." She'd been expecting an apology. Instead, Matthew was acting as though this was somehow *her* fault.

Or maybe he was still reeling from the news about her sterility. Since he already had children, she'd hoped it wouldn't be such a big deal to him. She should have known better. Men cared about stuff like this. Fertility was sexy. Sterility…just the opposite. With the experiences she'd had, she should have been more prepared.

She sank to the edge of the bed as she struggled to drag on her panty hose. Damn, she hated putting on hose that had already been worn. She paused for a moment, then rubbed her eyes. The back of her hand came away damp and smeared with mascara.

"Let this happen? I didn't—" Matt swore again. "I gave Derrick that key months ago, after I had the place decorated. I wanted him to feel welcome. But this is the first time he ever used it."

"Well, doesn't that just figure…"

"And things were just getting better between me and my son." Matthew stopped what he was doing and clutched his head between his hands.

Finally, Jane worked the hose past her thighs.

"I can't believe I was so stupid—"

As she left the room, she finished the sentence for him in her head.

"—*so stupid as to sleep with you.*"

In the living room she grabbed her jacket and slipped her feet into her heels. Her briefcase was on the floor next to Matthew's son's knapsack. He must have forgotten it in his hurry to get out of here.

Well, he wasn't the only one eager to make an escape. She stuffed her bra into the briefcase, then opened the front door.

"Jane?" Matthew called out. He was still in the bedroom. "Where are you going? I'm sorry if I—"

She left, shutting the door on the rest of his sentence.

MATTHEW HAD TO TALK to his son. Things were a mess with Jane, too, but Derrick was his first priority. He ran outside and checked up and down the street, but didn't see any sign of either Jane or Derrick.

He retrieved his car from underground parking and tried to think where to go first. Since it was almost six, it was a safe bet that Derrick would be expected home for dinner soon.

Matthew headed for his old neighborhood. He drove carefully, but his mind was overloaded by the events of the past hour. Making love with Jane, the news of her sterility, then Derrick's appearance and the shock on his face…

He'd handled the situation terribly, Matthew realized. He shouldn't have let either of them leave. Not Derrick and not Jane.

He owed them both an apology.

By the time he'd reached the familiar street where Gillian and the kids lived, Matthew's heart rate had finally settled back to normal and his chaotic thoughts had calmed. He stared at the familiar two-story house and wondered where his children were.

Violet was surely inside. Gillian had always been a stickler for eating exactly at six o'clock. But no way could Derrick have made it back this quickly using public transportation.

Matthew turned the car around and drove to the nearest bus stop. He didn't have to wait too long before a city bus appeared. Derrick was one of five passengers to get off at the stop. As his son shuffled despondently toward home, Matthew caught up to him.

"Good, Derrick, I'm glad I found you. We need to talk." He wasn't surprised when his son tried to run away. He passed Derrick the backpack he'd left at the apartment. "Please, son. Hear me out on this."

Derrick glared at him, fury, outrage and hurt all too visible in his young eyes. "You expect me to believe there was nothing going on back there?"

Matthew let out a long breath. "No. The situation was exactly how it looked. But—"

"Mom was right about you two all along." Derrick slipped the pack over his shoulders and kept walking.

"Right about what? What did your mother tell you?" Matthew asked as he hurried to keep up.

"You and that woman. You're having an affair."

"No. It's not an affair. I'm not married anymore, Derrick. You know the divorce became final last month."

"Right. So today was the first time."

"Actually, it was."

"Come on, Dad. I'm not *stupid*. She was in the car when you picked me up from school on Friday."

"We were working that day."

"Working? Is that what you call it?"

"Just stand still for a minute, would you? I can't talk to you this way."

"Don't you get it? I don't want to talk to you."

"Then why were you at my apartment? You must have had something on your mind. Maybe next time you could let me know when you're planning to visit."

Derrick gave him a scornful look. "You said I could drop in whenever. Besides, did you ever think to check your phone messages?"

Matthew remembered the call he'd ignored earlier at the bar. Damn it. Why hadn't he at least glanced at the display? He never would have disregarded a call from Derrick.

"So why did you want to see me?" he asked again.

At last Derrick stopped walking. "I heard something at school. Sarah was talking to a bunch of the older soccer guys. They were bragging about what they did to the coach's car. And then Sarah started complaining about her mom's boyfriend."

"Her mother has a boyfriend?" Even as he said that, he was thinking. This might account for the comings and goings at night from the Boutin house.

"Yeah, I guess so. Anyway, Sarah said he was a jerk, and I figured you should know."

"Did Sarah say why she thought he was a jerk?"

"Not really. Just that she wouldn't be alone in a room with him if she could help it."

"Interesting." Matthew wondered if the police knew about this boyfriend. He'd have to make sure they did. After days of everything going wrong for his client, here was a tiny ray of hope, finally.

He clasped his son on the shoulder. "Thanks for telling me this, Derrick."

"Forget about it. It isn't important."

Matthew was about to explain to him that it might turn out to be *very* important, when the front door opened and Gillian stuck out her head. "Derrick, there you are. I've been worried. Dinner's on the table."

"Sorry, Mom. I'll be right in."

His ex glanced at Matthew, but didn't acknowledge his presence, just went back inside, leaving the door ajar for Derrick.

"I've gotta go." His son's tone was suddenly belligerent again.

"Wait just one minute." Matthew tried to place a hand on his shoulder, but Derrick avoided the contact. "We were talking about something else."

"You mean *Jane?*" Sarcasm dripped from Derrick's tongue.

"Yes, Jane. She's someone I care about very much. It would mean a lot to me if you—and Violet—got along with her."

"You want me to *get along* with her?"

"At a minimum."

"Well, that's not going to happen."

"She's a very nice person."

"Oh, right. So nice she dates married men." He ran for the front door, started to slip inside.

"Derrick, wait. That's not fair and it's not what happened. I've already explained the truth to you."

"Even if it is, I don't care. I just don't like her, okay? And I never will!"

CHAPTER SEVENTEEN

MATTHEW STOOD AT his ex-wife's house for several minutes. He wanted to see his children. He needed to talk some sense into Derrick, and he'd love a little time with Violet. But he had no doubt that if he knocked on the door, Gillian wouldn't let him in.

He wished their relationship was more amicable. That they could be friends…for their children's sake. But he couldn't imagine that happening. Especially not now that he knew she'd purposefully prejudiced his son against him, telling Derrick her suspicions as if they were truth.

Last year, when Gillian had barged in on his lunch with Jane and hurled those crazy accusations at them, he'd been stunned. Not just by Gillian's nerve at creating such a public and ugly scene, but by the fact that she could seriously believe he was having an affair.

Anyone who understood what made him tick would know that he would never betray his wife and family that way. That Gillian could accuse him of an affair meant she didn't know him at all.

And she'd poisoned Derrick's opinion of him, too.

A father should be an example to his children.

Someone they could look up to and admire. Right now, it seemed that he would never be that person for Derrick and Violet.

Slowly, he headed back to where he'd parked the car. Once he was in the driver's seat, he pulled out his phone. There were no missed calls from Jane.

He needed to find her.

He got out his BlackBerry. She hadn't left a message. He skipped over a few from clients, then listened to the message Derrick had told him about.

"Hey, Dad, I heard something at school today that might help the case for Coach Keller. I'm coming over. Maybe we can have supper together, if Mom says it's okay. I'll call her from your place. See you soon."

Matthew replayed the message one more time before erasing it.

If only…

No. He couldn't waste time on regrets. He'd have another chance to deal with Derrick. Right now he had to talk to Jane.

He tried calling her at home, at the office, on her cell, but had to leave messages every time. Finally, he drove by her condo, but the lights were out.

He killed the engine and slumped back in his seat. The street was quiet and dark. Hartford felt very empty to him at that moment. Just like his job, his apartment, his life. Where to go? The evening loomed like a deep, dark cave. He tried calling his brothers, but both were away from their phones.

In desperation he drove to the office.

ONLY A FEW dedicated lawyers were still at work when Matthew used his key card to gain access to the twenty-eighth floor. He walked past the deserted reception area, down the corridor that led to Jane's office. And there she was, at her desk, typing rapidly at the computer keyboard. For a while he lingered, unnoticed, in the doorway.

She'd showered and changed since their lovemaking earlier. Gone were the smudges under her eyes, the rumpled clothing and tousled hair. Her long locks shone with fresh-washed cleanliness and her plain white shirt added to her wholesome appearance.

He was flooded with an urge to take her into his arms and hold her. Derrick's unexpected appearance had cheated them of any postcoital cuddling.

It had also interrupted an important conversation.

He cleared his throat so she would know he was there. Startled, she looked up. He wasn't encouraged by her reaction when she saw him.

Her expressive brown eyes grew large and wary.

"What are you doing here?" Her tone was clinical, especially when compared with the throaty noises she'd made when they were in bed. "New developments on the Keller case?"

He thought about the rumor from school that Derrick had told him about. Jane would be as intrigued about the mother perhaps having a boyfriend as he was. But that would have to wait.

"I'm sorry about what happened in my apartment earlier."

"Me, too," she said with feeling.

"Not about what happened between you and me," he clarified. "But for the interruption and the way I reacted to it."

Her gaze slid back to the computer screen. "How is Derrick? Have you talked to him?"

"He's upset." More like furious, but no sense getting into that. "But what about you? You ran off so quickly I didn't have a chance to talk to you."

"It seemed like a good idea to get out of there."

But Derrick had already left. So what she meant was she had wanted to get away from *him*.

"You're acting very distant."

Her laugh was short. "Under the circumstances, don't you think that's a good thing?"

"Maybe the circumstances, as you call them, were a little awkward and unfortunate, but what happened doesn't change anything between you and me."

"Your son walked in on us in bed. He knows we had sex."

"Yeah, well, believe it or not, kids do walk in on their parents now and then. It's not the end of the world."

"We aren't his parents. You're his father and I'm the woman he already blames for breaking up his family."

She sounded angry and sad at the same time, and she still wasn't meeting his eyes. Matthew stepped into the room. "You did not break up our family. I've told him that."

She bowed her head but didn't say anything.

He came around her desk and moved behind her chair. Tentatively, he put his hands on her shoulders. Lowering his head to hers, he whispered, "I wish I'd had more time to hold you. To tell you that I love you."

She stiffened. "You don't have to say that."

"You think I don't mean it?"

She shrugged.

Her muscles grew even tighter—he wasn't helping her relax at all. Reluctantly, he returned to the other side of the desk so he could at least look at her.

"I mean it. Jane, I told you from the beginning this thing between us isn't just about sex. At least, not for me."

He waited, wanting her to offer him…something. But she didn't. He could guess what was bothering her. "There was something else we didn't get to talk about."

Her body stilled, so he knew he had her attention.

"The sterility. What happened, Jane?"

He had to wait a few moments before she would meet his gaze. But when she spoke, she didn't pull any punches. "I had my ovaries removed the summer before I started law school."

He hadn't known what to expect. Certainly not this. "Why?"

"My family has a history of ovarian cancer. My mom died from it when I was in high school."

"Jane…"

She held up her hand, signaling that she didn't want his sympathy. "When my GP found a growth on one of my ovaries, it didn't look good. I'll spare you the technicalities, but I went into surgery knowing I would probably lose at least one ovary. In the end they had to remove both."

Jane told the story as dispassionately as if she were discussing a business transaction. But her deeper emotions were betrayed by her old nervous habit as she flipped her pen round and round in her fingers.

He didn't know what to say. "I'm sorry" was lame, but it was all he could manage.

"In a way I was relieved. It meant I didn't have to live in fear that I would die from the same disease my mother had."

But at such a young age, to be told you could never have children… It must have been devastating. "You seem to have come to terms with the situation."

"With my sterility?" Her smile was cold. "I've had a lot of time to get used to it."

"What about the boyfriend who convinced you to write the LSAT? Was he still in the picture at the time?"

"Before. Not after."

She'd implied that the relationship had ended because she'd been admitted to law school whereas her boyfriend hadn't. Matthew had a suspicion things had been more complicated than that. "The jerk."

"No. Not really. He knew he wanted children. I wouldn't have been happy if he'd tried to sacrifice that dream to be with me."

"Well, I already have children, so you don't need to worry about that in our case." He smiled, but she didn't respond.

"You're still young enough to have more children, Matt."

"Maybe. But I don't want more children. I'd rather have you."

"Don't…" She stopped speaking. Shook her head.

"What's the matter?" He hated this damn desk between them. Jane was using it like a shield and he wished he could understand why. She'd been so warm and giving this afternoon. How could Derrick's unexpected visit have changed things so much? "Why shouldn't I tell you how I feel?"

"Because it hurts too much. Matt, I don't think you should be in here."

"This is crazy. Three hours ago we were making love. It was one of the most beautiful experiences of my life. I could have sworn you felt the same way."

He could tell his words weren't changing anything with her. She shook her head again, as if rejecting everything he was saying to her.

"Do you know what I'm doing in the office so late tonight?"

Her question sounded defiant, and the switch in subject had his head spinning. "Did something happen with one of your clients?"

"No. I've been writing my letter of resignation."

"What? That's crazy."

"Read it." She shifted so he could have a clear view of her computer screen. The letter she was working on was addressed to the senior partners of Brandstrom and Norton and began: "It gives me great regret…" He didn't bother reading any further.

"Why, Jane?"

"Because I can't work in the same office as you anymore."

THERE. She'd told him. Jane waited, hoping she'd feel better now that the moment she'd dreaded was over, but she didn't.

Matt stood and leaned over her desk. He had the same firm set to his jaw that he did when he presented closing arguments in a criminal trial.

"We've already discussed this," he said. "Married people can work together. There's no law against it. In fact, I know several law partnerships where—"

"Married? Who said anything about marriage?"

"Where did you think we were headed? I don't want a love affair. I want a future together."

Jane put her head down on the desk. She didn't know how much more of this she could take. Didn't he realize what he was doing to her? How much willpower it demanded not to fall into his arms and let him hold her the way she longed to be held?

To give in was so tempting. He'd told her he loved her. Wanted to marry her. He didn't seem to care about the sterility that had ended the other two significant relationships in her life.

Yet when she tried to believe that she and Matt could be happy together, she kept remembering Derrick's face—every time he met her.

"What about your son? He *hates* me, Matt."

"Derrick's angry and confused right now. But he'll get over it."

"What if he doesn't?"

"He will."

"You can't be sure. The two of you already have so many problems to deal with. You were just starting to get along. I can't stand in the way of you and your children."

"What do I have to say to convince you? You're not."

She resumed typing. She only had one more line, then the closing. When she finished, she hit Print.

"Jane. Don't. You're making a mistake."

She reached over to the printer and grabbed the paper while it was still warm to the touch. "I told you. I'm resigning."

"No. I won't allow you—"

"You can't stop me." She signed the letter, folded it and slipped it into an envelope. She expected Matthew to leave, but he wasn't moving. Having him watch her was unnerving. She turned her back to him as she printed off a second copy of the letter for her records.

"So you're really walking out on me?"

She didn't think of it that way. She was stepping aside for him. Once she was out of the competition, he would definitely be chosen for the senior partner. He could mend his relationship with his son. Move on with his life.

He might be angry now, but later, when he'd had a

chance to think things through, he'd realize she'd done the best thing.

"What about your clients? Are you leaving them in the lurch, too?"

"I'm not leaving *anyone* in the lurch. Least of all my clients." She would go over her list of outstanding cases with Eve and Russell tomorrow. Some could be easily reassigned. Others she would follow through to completion.

Briefly, she wondered what she would do with herself once she'd left Brandstrom and Norton. Begin phoning colleagues, she supposed. Somewhere in the city of Hartford would be the right job for her.

If not, she could always relocate.

"I wonder how Wally Keller will feel about this."

Something in Matthew's voice hinted that he had more to say. "Why bring up that particular case?" she asked.

"There's been a development."

She could tell it was a biggie. "Oh?"

"Derrick mentioned that some kids at school heard Sarah talking about her mom's secret boyfriend."

"What do you mean by *secret?*"

"No one knows about him. I'm not sure why. But apparently, Sarah doesn't like him very much."

Jane stared at him thoughtfully. They both knew that in cases of abuse when the victim came from a broken home, the mother's boyfriend was often to blame.

In fact, some sickos preyed on single mothers with attractive adolescent daughters just for this reason.

"If her mom does have a boyfriend, the police should question him."

"I agree. Tomorrow I'm going to talk to the officer in charge about it." Matt hesitated a moment. "Want to come with me?"

Spend more time with him? She shook her head, knowing she couldn't handle that. Not yet.

Maybe not ever.

THE DETECTIVE ASSIGNED to Sarah Boutin's case agreed to meet at a downtown coffee shop the next morning. As he headed toward the meeting location, Matthew rubbed his jaw, feeling the results of his poor efforts at shaving that morning.

He'd had a lousy night's sleep and he'd hardly been able to face himself in the mirror after his shower. He'd screwed up with Jane so badly. He couldn't believe she was resigning. Leaving the firm.

Because of him.

He couldn't let it happen.

The Coffee Stop was a favorite haunt of Hartford police. He'd met Nick here many times and couldn't help but check for his brother as he entered the cozy café. The air was redolent with the enticing combination of fresh baked goods and strong black coffee.

Nick wasn't there, of course. Matthew made a note to call him later. If his brother was serious about getting married, it was time for the family to meet this Jessica. Their mother would be excited by the prospect of another wedding. Not to mention another grandchild.

Babies were springing up everywhere in the Gray family these days, it seemed. How would that have made Jane feel? God, it must have been hard for her over the years to be surrounded by friends and colleagues having babies, all the while knowing it would never be possible for her....

But he didn't want to feel sorry for Jane now. He was still pissed at her. If she didn't love him, fine. But to actually quit her job. That was going too far. If she'd set out to make him feel guilty, she'd done a fine job of it.

Matthew lined up to order coffee, then took his cup to a table near the entrance. Five minutes later Detective Harold Green walked in, dressed in a golf shirt tucked neatly into pressed khakis. He looked like the kind of cop who crossed his t's and dotted his i's.

Matthew stood to shake his hand. "I would have bought you a coffee, but I didn't know what you liked in it."

"Sometimes I think I'm the only North American who drinks plain black coffee anymore. But that's okay. I've already had plenty." He sat in the empty chair, shifting it a little so that he could see the entrance.

Matthew smiled. "My brother does that, too."

"Huh?" The detective paused in the act of pulling out his notebook.

"My brother always sits so he can watch the customers come and go. He's a cop, too."

"Ah. You must mean Nick Gray. Good man."

Matthew could tell he'd just gone up a notch in the detective's estimation. Great; he'd take his advantages where he could get them.

"The reason I wanted to talk to you was to ask about the victim's mother's boyfriend."

"Claudia Boutin doesn't have a boyfriend. She's going through a messy separation right now."

Bingo. He hadn't known. "Isn't the Boutins' divorce final?" Matthew asked, feigning ignorance.

"Not by a long shot. Those two are fighting about everything from money, to custody, to division of household assets." The detective's pale eyebrows shifted closer together. "What makes you think Mrs. Boutin has a boyfriend?"

"My son, Derrick, goes to the same school as Sarah. He heard her complaining about some guy her mother has been dating. She says the relationship is secret. Also, she doesn't appear to like the guy very much."

"Sarah said nothing about this to us. *Nobody* said anything about this to us." Harold Green leaned back, eyeing Matthew speculatively.

"Maybe it's just a rumor. But it should be investigated. One of the next-door neighbors told me she's heard a lot of late-night activity at the Boutin residence. Cars coming and going. Doors slamming. That sort of thing."

"You've got your ear to the ground on this one."

"He was a good coach. Went out of his way to help the kids."

The detective sighed. "Okay. We'll check the boyfriend angle. But, damn it. I hate cases like this where

all you have to go on is what people decide to tell you.
I prefer cold hard facts myself."

"I don't blame you."

"You know, we were planning to arrest your client
today."

"So I heard."

"I guess we'll hold off on that until I check this
out."

"Thanks."

The detective rose from his chair. "My partner and
I will head over to the Boutins' this afternoon."

"You'll let me know what you find?"

"You bet. Thanks for passing this on," Green said,
as he made his way to the door. But from the look on
his face as he exited, he didn't seem all that grateful.

CHAPTER EIGHTEEN

"I CAN'T BELIEVE THIS." Eve Brandstrom tossed Jane's sealed letter onto Russell Fielding's desk, clearly annoyed. She crossed the room and stared out at the view. Jane didn't think she was seeing a blessed thing.

As usual, the older woman looked professional and elegant. Her dark brown bob was sleek, her makeup flawless, and her designer suit showed off a still-shapely figure.

Over the years Jane had heard rumors of the men who had fallen for beautiful and brilliant Eve Brandstrom. She'd spurned them all. Eve's relationships were only transient. Her true love was her job.

"Is this what we think it is?" From his seat behind his desk, Russell poked the envelope, then peered at Jane. He seemed to be silently begging her to tell him he was wrong.

Jane, feet planted firmly on the thick carpet, didn't budge. "It's my letter of resignation."

"This is indiscreet of me to say, but you were one of our top two candidates for senior partner." Russell tented his hands before glancing back at her to assess the impact his pronouncement had on her decision.

"I appreciate that, Russell. But it doesn't change my mind."

"This is about Gray, isn't it?" Eve whirled to face the room again. Her smoky eyes were dark, her red lips taut with anger.

"I'd rather not say."

"Damn it, Jane. You've worked too hard to throw your career away for a man. In the end, you'll regret it—I promise you. Oh, maybe the marriage will be fun for a while. But in the long run, a career is a better investment than a man."

"Matthew and I are not getting married."

"What?" Both Russell and Eve seemed startled. Then puzzled. "Then why, Jane?" Russell asked, his tone almost gentle, "Why are you leaving us?"

He made it sound so personal. Actually, both senior partners were taking her resignation that way. Which was making this even harder than she'd anticipated.

Jane pressed her lips together. These people were more than mentors. They were family. She knew Russell's wife and children. She and Eve shared season symphony tickets.

"I'm sorry. I've loved working here. I've learned so much and enjoyed every minute of it. But I can't stay anymore. It's—impossible."

For a long moment there was silence. Then Eve sighed. "You must love him very much."

Jane blinked away a tear. This was not the time. She raised her chin. "As I said, I'm not comfortable discussing this." She patted the letter, reminding them of its presence. "Everything that needs to be said is in here. Of course I'll make sure all my files are properly taken care of."

"Including the Keller case?" Eve asked.

"Matthew can handle that on his own." He could have from the start. They'd both been assigned to the case as a test.

A test she had failed.

She turned to leave, but Russell's voice stopped her.

"At least sleep on this, Jane."

"Yes," Eve added. "We'll hold on to your letter for a week. At any time during those seven days you can change your mind. If we don't hear from you by next Thursday, we'll open the letter. Fair enough?"

"More than fair." Jane hurried out the room, headed blindly for her office. This wasn't the time to cry. But she was doing so anyway.

AFTER A CRAZY DAY in court, Matthew closed the door to his office, desperate for some peace and quiet. Quickly, he checked his phone messages and e-mail. Wally Keller appeared eager to talk to him. But there was no word from his son. And nothing from Jane.

He removed his glasses and rubbed the bridge of his nose.

His head still pounded.

He called reception. "Is Jane Prentice in her office?"

"She hasn't been in since this morning. Russell told me she's on a one-week vacation."

Vacation? What about her letter of resignation? He tried her home number again, then the cell. *Damn it. Answer, Jane.* But she didn't.

He drank some of the coffee he'd ordered downstairs. If he was going to deal with the twenty urgent phone calls logged into his message center, he needed the caffeine.

First, he dialed Detective Green, using speakerphone so he could simultaneously sort through the papers that had landed on his desk that day.

"This is Matthew Gray, Detective. We spoke this morning at the—"

"Right." Green required no further reminder. "I thought I should fill you in on what happened when my partner and I went to visit Claudia Boutin this afternoon."

"I appreciate that."

"We arrived at the Boutin residence at approximately one-thirty, only to find that the rumored boyfriend was a flesh-and-blood reality. He's eight years Mrs. Boutin's junior, with a list of priors that would make your skin crawl."

Hearing it, Matthew's skin *did* crawl.

"At first Mrs. Boutin didn't want to believe the guy had a record. She told us we had the wrong man. She'd met the boyfriend at her gym. As far as she was concerned this was love. She told us the boyfriend was never around her children. He couldn't possibly have hurt Sarah. Besides, he wouldn't. He loved her too much."

"The power of denial." Matthew had seen it in action many, many times.

"No kidding. This woman was a classic case. She stuck by that guy until the kids got home from school. Sarah took one look at us, one look at the boyfriend, then burst into tears. I tell you, it was heartbreaking."

For a hardened detective to say that, Matthew could only imagine how intense the scene had been. "Poor kid."

"That's for sure. She was too upset to give us a statement, but she did clear your client."

Matthew felt glad for Coach Keller. "So you're dropping the case against him?"

"We are."

Thank goodness for small miracles, Matthew thought, as they concluded their call. Wally Keller had been innocent after all.

He let that sink in for a minute. Yet it wouldn't feel real until he told Jane. If only she would answer his call. Where was she? Was it possible she really had left town on some sort of impromptu vacation?

He was picking up his phone, planning to try all her numbers again, when it rang. He hit the talk button hopefully, then saw from call display that Wally Keller was phoning.

"Wally? Have you heard the good news?" He listened for several minutes as his client vented his relief, his anger, his confusion and his gratitude.

"Thank you so much for helping me with this, Matthew. You and Jane Prentice are quite a team."

Hearing his name linked to Jane's, even professionally, made his heart ache. "Glad we could be of service. So will your wife be returning home soon?"

Wally's tone became uncertain. "I hope so. I haven't been able to talk to her. This…business… It's been hard on her. Dredged up a lot of unhappy memories about what happened in Maine. This was supposed to be our fresh start."

"I'm sorry." Matthew had witnessed other clients go through the same whirlwind of emotions. Having the system clear you of wrongdoing was wonderful. Unfortunately, the stigma of having been suspected in the first place seemed to stick. Even if the true villain was eventually prosecuted and found guilty, it was unlikely that the West Hartford community where he and his family had once been accepted so easily would ever be quite as warm and friendly.

"Keep calling her," Matthew advised. "The two of you should talk."

"You're right. I will," Wally assured him.

He hung up, knowing that the same advice applied to Jane and him. They had to talk. If only he could find her.

She could be at the gym. That was one of her favorite places to unwind. Or maybe she was at Sully's, having drinks with Liam James. The very idea made Matthew's gut burn.

He wished he had the time to track her down. But

this was his night with Violet and he simply couldn't miss it. He locked up his office, then headed for his car. The timing was tight, so he skipped his usual burger drive-through and managed to arrive at his ex-wife's house just before she had to leave.

"I thought maybe you'd forgotten." Gillian was in the foyer, already slipping on her jacket.

He could hear the TV going in the family room. "Is Violet in there?"

"Yes. Derrick's at soccer practice. He'll be home in half an hour. His dinner is waiting in the fridge."

Matthew's stomach rumbled at the mention of food. Gillian must have heard, because she added, "There's enough for you, too, if you're hungry."

"Thanks." The offer surprised him. He gave his ex a closer look. "Everything okay?"

"Sure." Then in an offhand tone she added, "I heard about Claudia Boutin's boyfriend."

Ah. All of a sudden, he understood her change in attitude.

"So, Coach Keller...he's off the hook?" Gillian studied one of the bold black buttons of her coat.

"That's right. The police won't be laying any charges." Did she feel badly for berating him about the case? Matthew wondered.

"He must be relieved. Life can go back to normal."

"I'm not sure anything will feel normal for the Kellers. Not for a long while."

"I did hear that his wife and kids had left."

Their eyes met, and he wondered if she was thinking

the same thing he was. That once a family was torn asunder, piecing it back together was damn hard. Especially in the Kellers' situation, where they were in crisis mode for the second time in as many years.

"Well…" Gillian cleared her throat. "I'd better get going. It doesn't do for the teacher to be late."

On impulse Matthew asked, "Do you ever think about returning to acting?"

Yearning flashed over her face before she shook her head. "Violet's so young."

"She's not a baby anymore. We have options. Day care. Nursery school."

"True." She hesitated, then blurted, "Actually, Peter Kenyon approached me last month. Do you remember him?"

Matthew nodded. He was the director in residence for a local theater company.

"Peter wants me to audition for the part of the wealthy widow in *Suddenly, Last Summer.*"

"You've always loved Tennessee Williams."

"Yes. But it would be a huge time commitment, including a lot of late evenings."

"I could help out more." Even as he made the offer, Matthew thought about the senior partnership. If he was chosen, more would be expected of him at the office. Could he deliver all that, plus spend extra time with the kids?

Gillian looked ready to scoff. Then she surprised him with that yearning look again. "Do you really think you could?"

"We can work something out," he said firmly. "You should consider it, Gillian. You've put your career on the back burner for a long time."

"Maybe I will." She stunned him with a smile. The first genuine smile from his ex-wife that he'd had in a long while.

Maybe an amicable relationship between the two of them wasn't as impossible as he had thought.

AS USUAL, spending the evening with his daughter helped Matthew appreciate the things that had gone right with his life. After her bedtime story Violet fell fast asleep. He pulled up her covers, then brushed the hair back from her face. Not that long ago, she'd been wearing diapers and sleeping in a crib. Before he knew it, she'd be in first grade.

He sat on the edge of her bed, basking in the quiet joy of being her father. The promise he'd made to Gillian felt better than ever as he watched her sleep. He'd missed out on a lot of these moments with Derrick. Matthew was determined to make up for those lapses. As much as he could.

Eventually, his thoughts turned to Jane, and he felt a deep sorrow. She would never have this, never experience the deep, fulfilling love of a parent for a child.

He felt the enormity of her loss, with a depth that put tears in his eyes. In some ways having that operation must have been like aging thirty years in one day. She'd gone to sleep a young, fertile woman, a woman with at least some hope of having a family of her own one day.

She'd awoken to find all that hope and potential taken from her.

He couldn't imagine how difficult adjusting must have been. And on top of it all, her boyfriend had dumped her, leaving scars just as real as those sutured so neatly by the surgeon.

No children for Jane. No husband, either. She'd ended up throwing all her passion into her work. She was an excellent lawyer. One of the very best. She'd earned her junior partnership years earlier than most, and now she was practically a shoo-in for the senior partnership.

Only, she was giving that up. Giving up all she'd worked for since she'd passed the bar.

For him.

Matthew dropped his head into his hands. He couldn't let her do this. If she didn't want to be with him, fine. But she couldn't be the one who sacrificed her career.

It had to be him.

As soon as he'd made the decision, it felt right. He'd resign from the partnership and start work on his own so he could control his hours and make more time for the kids.

Jane would stay at Brandstrom and Norton. She would get the promotion to senior partner that she deserved.

It was the only just way.

Feeling better than he had in days, Matthew kissed

Violet's forehead, then left the room. Was it too late to call Russell or Eve? Now that his mind was made up, he wanted to act.

He'd left his jacket on one of the kitchen chairs, but as he went to pull out his cell phone, the back door opened. Derrick was home. Matthew heard the sound of shoes being kicked off, a gym bag landing on the floor. His son came into the kitchen.

Derrick froze for a second when he spotted his father. Then he went to the fridge and pulled out a carton of juice.

"How was practice?" Matthew left his phone where it was. His call would have to wait until tomorrow.

"It sucked." Derrick opened the fridge again for the dinner his mother had waiting. He put it into the microwave oven to warm up, and soon the scents of chili and garlic toast were making Matthew's mouth water.

"Is there any more of that?"

Derrick found a large storage container filled with leftovers and silently passed it to him.

"Thanks." Matthew waited for his turn with the microwave. "So what was the problem at practice?"

"We didn't do anything. The new coach didn't have any drills for us to work on or any plays for us to practice. We just goofed around the whole time."

Matthew searched his son's face for signs that Derrick blamed him for not volunteering for the coaching position. Not that he was any expert, but he would have been able to put the boys to work on the field tonight, at least.

There was no sign that Derrick was feeling resentful. He carried his plate to the kitchen counter, climbed up on a stool and started eating. A minute later, Matthew joined him.

They ate in quiet companionship, which was a nice change. Derrick's anger from the previous day seemed to have vanished, and later, when they were having ice cream for dessert, Matthew finally understood why.

"Robert Boutin wasn't at practice tonight." Derrick threw the news out casually, but Matthew could tell it was important.

"I guess there's a lot going on in his life," he replied diplomatically.

"Is it true that the police arrested his mom's boyfriend for what happened to Sarah?"

"Yes."

"Why did Sarah say it was Coach Keller if it wasn't?"

"Kids get scared. They don't always do the logical thing."

"Everyone on the team thought you were wrong to defend Coach Keller. But you turned out to be right."

For the first time in a long while Matthew's son was looking up to him, the way he had as a child, in the days when his father had been the ultimate authority on the world.

Having his approval for a change felt wonderful. But Matthew knew he had to be up front. "In this case my client was innocent, yes. But there are times when the people I defend are guilty. I have to do my best for my clients no matter what."

Derrick didn't seem to care about the theoretical. All that mattered was this one case in particular. "Do you think Daniel Keller will move back to Hartford and his dad will coach the team again?"

"I'm not sure what the Kellers will decide to do. I doubt if Wally Keller will be your coach again, though."

"Why? He was innocent, right?"

Matthew sighed. "Have you heard the expression 'Too much water under the bridge'?"

"Yeah. That's what Mom said when I asked her if you guys would ever get back together."

Matthew closed his eyes. The resignation in Derrick's voice told him everything about how this divorce had affected his son. Matthew's earlier resolve returned. More than ever, he knew that what he was planning to do was the right thing.

CHAPTER NINETEEN

DID DRINKING IN A BAR full of strangers still qualify as drinking alone?

Wait a minute. She knew the bartender. His name was Stewart.

Jane called his name and was gratified when he came immediately, understanding without her having to say a word that she wanted a refill of the merlot.

"Thank you, Stewart."

"My pleasure, Jane."

She smiled. He knew her name, too. So they definitely weren't strangers. She took a sip from her glass. Was it her third or her fourth? She'd sipped the first one slowly, with the idea of making it last until she was ready to go home.

But when the glass was empty, she still wasn't ready.

The problem was, she had nowhere to go. She couldn't go to the office. She didn't work there anymore.

She, Jane Marie Prentice, was no longer a partner at Brandstrom and Norton. Oh, sure, she had that one-week cooling off period Russell and Eve had insisted on during their meeting on Monday, but that was just a technicality. For all intents and purposes, she was unemployed.

So what the heck was she supposed to do with herself now? Apply for another job, obviously. Over the years she'd had offers. All she had to do was pull out her stash of business cards and pick a name.

But the idea of phoning those people, asking for interviews and starting fresh at a brand-new law firm, filled her with despair.

She didn't want to work anywhere else. Maybe she'd never had children, but she was godmother to the office manager's daughter. Would they stay in touch if she left the firm? And what about Susan? Who would she complain to now about her crazy home life?

And then there was Matthew.

She'd never loved any man the way she loved him. She couldn't believe that she'd finally severed the one tie between them.

She'd had to do it. She simply wasn't strong enough to continue working with a man she loved with all her heart but couldn't have.

Quitting had been her only option. Only, now she wondered if she might have to move, too. The Hartford legal community wasn't that large. Eventually, she would run into Matthew. It might happen next week in court—or it might happen now in Sully's Tavern.

He was here.

She hadn't noticed him arrive, but she could see his

face clearly, reflected in the mirror behind the bar. Holding her breath, she watched as he walked toward her. His expression made her tense anxiously. He looked concerned about something.

She stiffened, preparing herself for the moment he said her name.

"Jane."

She longed to hurl herself into his arms. Instead, she gripped her wineglass tighter. It was empty. How had that happened?

"You haven't answered any of my calls." He removed her purse from the stool beside her so that he could sit there.

"Thath's because I didn't think we should talk." She wouldn't turn her head. Wouldn't look at him.

"Jane, you're slurring your words. How much wine have you had?"

"Not your concern." That sounded rude. Almost mean. She didn't want to be like this with Matthew, but she was afraid to be herself, to let her true feelings surface.

"I have something to tell you. Would you look at me, please?"

For an answer, she buried her face in her hands. "Just leave me alone."

"Oh, Jane."

There was so much feeling in his voice it made her want to cry. Why did the one man she connected with, the one man who didn't seem to care that she couldn't have children...why did he have to be the guy she couldn't have?

She needed to strengthen her resolve, so she thought about Derrick. Every time he saw her, his young face tightened with bitterness and resentment. Matthew claimed it didn't matter, but Jane knew better.

Matthew's children were everything to him. And that was the way it ought to be.

She picked up her purse from where Matthew had placed it on the counter. With fingers less coordinated than usual, she counted out some money.

"What are you doing?"

"This is for my good friend Stewart." She tucked the cash next to her empty wineglass, then slid off her stool. For a moment she wobbled on her heels. *That's funny. The floor was level when I walked in here.*

"Don't go. I need to tell you something."

Ignore him. She tucked her purse close to her body, then eyed the exit. All she had to do was remain upright until she got out to the street. Once she was safely in the backseat of a cab, she could fall apart.

She managed her first step.

"Jane. I quit my job."

She stopped. "What?" She looked back at him. What he'd said was so outrageous she couldn't help herself.

"I handed Russell and Eve my letter of resignation today."

She struggled to make sense of this. "But why? You're going to be senior partner."

"No. *You're* going to be senior partner. You deserve it more than I do."

"That isn't true." Matthew was a top-notch attorney. Why had he done this? He'd been working at the firm just as long as she had. Plus, he had children to support.

"It's done. I've resigned. You've got to go back. The firm needs you. Russell and Eve told me about the one-week grace period. Tomorrow you can tell them that you changed your mind and you've decided to stay."

She stared at him a long time, working this out in her head. Finally, she understood. He was making her a gift. Not the one she wanted most, but the only one he could give her.

The question was, should she accept it?

He seemed to understand her struggle. Firmly, he nodded. "Go back to them, Jane. It's the right thing to do. No matter what, I'm out of there. I've decided to work on my own and spend more time with the kids. I've promised Gillian. It's a done deal."

His decision shocked Jane. She was glad that he was making Derrick and Violet a bigger priority in his life, but he'd been so ambitious, just like her.

Could he really change his life so dramatically? "You're certain?"

"Absolutely."

She let that word sink in. Once she'd accepted that this was his decision, her path was clear. "Okay. I'll go back."

"Thank you."

She nodded, then headed for the exit once more. This time Matthew didn't call out to stop her. Five minutes later she was in the backseat of a cab. A strand of worry beads dangled from the car's rearview mirror, and she watched them shift with the movements of the steering wheel.

She had her career back. She ought to be thankful.

Instead, she couldn't help wishing that rather than telling her about his resignation, Matthew had tracked her down to confess that he couldn't live without her.

ONE MONTH LATER Matthew was surprised to receive an invitation to dinner from Gillian. Sitting at the kitchen table with his kids and his ex-wife was kind of strange. But kind of nice, too.

He and Derrick were getting along better these days, though lately Derrick had been lobbying hard—and unsuccessfully—for an extension to his weekend curfew.

"My friends get to stay out past ten…"

"Sorry, Derrick. Your mom and I have talked about this and your curfew won't be changing until you're in high school."

"Can I have some milk, Daddy?"

"Sure, honey." He filled Violet's glass, then Derrick's, while Gillian set the casserole she'd prepared on the table.

"Smells great." He was about to reach over to serve the kids, when Gillian raised her glass of water, as if it were wine.

"I have an announcement."

His stomach tightened. What kind of bomb was she going to drop now?

But it turned out to be good news.

"I got the part! Your mommy is officially an actor again."

They all cheered. "That's fabulous, Gillian. You should have warned me. I would have brought champagne. And you should have invited Bruce. We could have made this a party."

"Bruce?" Gillian looked at him as though he was clueless. "I haven't seen him in over a month. I'm dating Peter now."

"Not the director?"

"Yes."

"Is that a good idea?"

"Probably not." She shrugged. "But when we ran into each other again, we just knew it was the right thing."

He could relate to that.

"It's not why I got the part," she added sharply.

"I never thought it was."

"Are you going to be on TV, Mommy?"

"No. On the stage. I'll need to work very hard and put in lots of hours." She glanced over at Matthew. "You'll be spending more time at Dad's place."

Violet reacted with a big smile, but Matthew could tell Derrick had his doubts. Later, when Violet was in her room, putting on her pajamas, he asked his son if he was okay with the changes taking place lately.

"Yeah, I guess so." Then Derrick surprised him by asking, "What about you? Do you like working on your own?"

"It's good for now," Matthew answered honestly.

"Really? 'Cause you don't seem that happy. I even heard Mom say so when she was talking to one of her friends on the phone."

He'd been pretty low, he knew, but he hadn't realized it was noticeable. "Any new business takes a while to get started. I don't have many clients yet, but that will change."

"Okay," Derrick murmured, but he didn't sound convinced.

Matthew wasn't sure what else he could say to reassure him. He was actually enjoying operating as a one-man law firm. Missing Jane was what was getting him down.

But he couldn't tell Derrick that.

WHEN A WRAPPED BOX of specialty chocolate-chip cookies arrived at the office the day after her promotion to senior partner, Jane didn't need to open the card to know the cookies were from Matthew.

She opened the card anyway, hoping to find at least a small personal message from him. But all he'd written was, "You deserve it. Matt."

With her appointment had come a move to one of the corner offices. She was sitting there now, in the new leather chair purchased in her chosen shade of apricot.

The congratulatory cocktail party the firm had thrown for her in the conference room was over now. It was time to go home. She closed her eyes tightly, then opened them fast.

She was still here, in the corner office, in the leather chair. She smiled and twirled the chair. This felt great. It really did.

Only…

Her gaze fell on the box of cookies. He'd bought her favorite kind.

No. She shouldn't be thinking about Matthew. She should go out and celebrate. She could call Liam James. He'd left her a few messages that she'd never returned. Or she could drop in at Sully's and see if she spotted a familiar face.

Jane grabbed her briefcase and, after a moment's consideration, the box of cookies, too. She locked her new office, then made her way to the elevators. The place was deserted. She must have been sitting in her office longer than she'd realized.

Out on the street, the sun was blazing. Spring had led to summer and the city was experiencing its first heat wave. She removed her jacket, then undid the top button of her blouse.

Unexpectedly she thought about Matthew at Sully's, getting all jealous because she'd had dinner with Liam. Another memory—Matthew undoing her buttons at his apartment, the one and only time they'd made love. Jane smiled, even though she felt sad, and kept walking.

Eventually, she found herself at a corner. If she turned right, she'd be at Sully's Tavern. To the left was Bushnell Park.

The day was so beautiful. To head to a dark, noisy tavern seemed a pity. She turned left.

She walked until she saw an empty park bench, then sat down and ate a cookie.

Butter, sugar, chocolate…blended to perfection. Much better than a glass of wine, she decided. She ate another. When that was gone, she reached into the box again.

"You'd better be careful. You're going to make yourself sick."

She was so surprised she dropped the box to the grass. Cookies tumbled out, spilling everywhere.

But all she could focus on was Matt.

"How did you get here?"

"I was at Sully's. Hoping you would show up. I was sitting at the window, and saw you walk this way."

She'd never seen him looking better. Did that mean his new life was agreeing with him? Or just that she'd missed him so much the sight of him was making her giddy? Actually, when she examined him closer, she thought he'd lost some weight. "Thank you for the cookies."

"Forget about the cookies."

"Pardon?"

"I'm not here to congratulate you, if that's what you think." He held out his hands. Without pause, she placed hers in them. He pulled her to her feet, facing him. Then closer.

"I've decided you were using Derrick as an excuse."

"Pardon me?" she asked again.

"You were afraid of loving me. Even more, you were afraid of letting me love you."

"That's not true! I *was* worried about your children." How could he doubt her motives? Did he really believe that fear would have stood in her way?

Her chest tightened. She felt the urge to run. To deny. No. What he was saying couldn't be right.

"Derrick is just a child," Matthew said. "He's gone through a lot since the divorce. But you're a wonderful person. With patience and lots of understanding, I know Derrick will appreciate that one day."

Matthew sounded so positive. For a moment she allowed herself to hope. Then the fear slammed into her again. No. Happily ever after didn't happen for people like her. "And if he doesn't?"

"I don't for a minute believe that's a possibility. He's a good kid, Jane."

"Like his dad," she whispered.

"We've had a hard road. But things will get better. We belong together. I've never been so sure of that as I am now after all this time apart. I don't want to be without you anymore. So what do you say, Jane? Will you marry me?"

He pressed her to him until she could feel the thumping of his heart and the power of his gaze.

"Marry…?" Her voice squeaked. "But I'm—"

"It doesn't matter that you can't have babies. It doesn't matter to me, anyway," he amended. "Two children is plenty."

She shook her head. "Men care about stuff like that. Even if they think they don't want any more children, no man wants a wife who's—"

"Stop." He gave her a little shake. "Don't you dare say one negative word about the woman I love."

She thought he was going to argue with her some more, but he didn't. He kissed her.

The connection between them was strong as ever. She wanted to lead him to her bed. Unfortunately, they were standing in the middle of the park with a handful of passersby watching them curiously.

"Did she say yes yet?" one old man asked.

"Come on, lady," said his buddy. "You're breaking his heart."

The old man raised his voice. "You're breaking *my* heart. Say yes, lady. Say *yes.*"

"Yes." The word blurted out. Later she would say the old guys had been badgering the witness. Now all she felt was a quiet certainty that she'd found the right man to trust with her heart.

Within seconds, Matthew was on his knees.

"You don't have to do that," she said. "It's just a silly old custom."

"What? I was picking up the cookies."

She laughed, then sank to the ground to help him. He certainly had his priorities straight. After all this time, they both did.

* * * * *

*Mills & Boon® Special Moments™
brings you a sneak preview.*

In Mistletoe and Miracles *child psychologist
Trent Marlowe can't believe his eyes when Laurel
– the woman he'd loved and lost – comes to him for
help. Now a widow with a troubled son, Laurel needs
a miracle from Trent...and a brief detour under the
mistletoe wouldn't hurt either...*

*Turn the page for a peek at this fantastic new story
from Marie Ferrarella, available next month in
Mills & Boon® Special Moments™!*

*Don't forget you can still find all your favourite
Superromance and Special Edition stories
every month in Special Moments™!*

Mistletoe and Miracles
by
Marie Ferrarella

For a moment, Trent Marlowe thought he was dreaming.

When he first looked up from the latest article on se-lective mutism and saw her standing in the doorway of his office, he was certain he had fallen asleep.

But even though the article was dry, the last time he'd actually nodded out while sitting at a desk had been during an eight-o'clock Pol-Sci 1 class, where the lack-luster professor's monotone voice had been a first-class cure for insomnia.

He'd been a college freshman then.

And so had she.

Blinking, Trent glanced down at his appointment calendar and then up again at the sad-eyed, slender blonde. It was nine in the morning and he had a full day ahead of him, beginning with a new patient, a Cody Greer. Cody was only six years old and was brought in by his mother, Laurel Greer.

When he'd seen it on his schedule, the first name had given him a fleeting moment's pause. It made him remember another Laurel. Someone who had been a very important part of his life. But that was years ago and if he thought of her every now and then, it was never in this setting. Never walking into his office. After all, like his stepmother, he had become a child psychologist, and Laurel Valentine was hardly a child. Even when she'd been one.

Laurel wasn't that unusual a name. It had never occurred to him that Laurel Greer and Laurel Valentine were one and the same person.

And yet, here she was, in his doorway. Just as achingly beautiful as ever.

Maybe more so.

Trent didn't remember rising from behind his desk. Didn't remember opening his mouth to speak. His voice sounded almost surreal to his ear as he said her name. "Laurel?"

And then she smiled.

It was a tense, hesitant smile, but still Laurel's smile, splashing sunshine through the entire room. That was when he knew he wasn't dreaming, wasn't revisiting a space in his mind reserved for things that should have been but weren't.

Laurel remained where she was, as if she had doubts about taking this last step into his world. "Hello, Trent. How are you?"

Her voice was soft, melodic. His was stilted. "Startled."

He'd said the first word that came to him. But this wasn't a word association test. Trent laughed dryly to shake off the bewildered mood that closed around him.

How long had it been? Over seven years now. And, at first glance, she hadn't changed. She still had a shyness that made him think of a fairy-tale princess in need of rescue.

Confusion wove its way through the moment. Had she come here looking for him? Or was it his professional services she needed? But he didn't treat adults.

"I'm a child psychologist," he heard himself telling her.

Her smile widened, so did the radiance. But that could have just been a trick of the sunshine streaming in the window behind him.

"I know," she said. "I have a child."

Something twisted inside of him, but he forced himself to ignore it. Trent tilted his head slightly as he looked behind her, but there didn't seem to be anyone with Laurel, at least not close by. Trent raised an inquiring eyebrow as his eyes shifted back to her.

"He's at home," she explained. "With my mother."

He looked at his watch even though three minutes ago he'd known what time it was. Right now he wasn't sure of anything. The ground had opened up beneath him and he'd fallen down the rabbit hole.

"Shouldn't he be in school?"

Laurel sighed before answering, as if some burden had made her incredibly tired. "These days, he doesn't want to go anymore." Laurel pressed her lips together and looked at him hopefully. "Can I come in?"

Idiot, Trent berated himself. But the sight of his first, no, his *only* love after all these years had completely thrown him for a loop, incinerating his usual poise.

He forced himself to focus. To relax. With effort, he locked away the myriad questions popping up in his brain.

"Of course. Sorry. Seeing you just now really caught me off guard." He gestured toward the two chairs before his sleek, modern desk. "Please, take a seat."

She moved across the room like the model she had once confided she wanted to become, gliding gracefully into one of the chairs he'd indicated. Placing her purse on the floor beside her, she crossed her ankles and folded her hands in her lap.

She seemed uncomfortable and she'd never been ill at ease around him before. But there were seven years between then and now. A lot could have happened in that time.

"I wanted to talk to you about Cody before you started working with him, but I didn't want him to hear me."

Did she think the boy wouldn't understand? Or that Cody would understand all too well? "Why?"

"Cody's practically a statue as it is. I don't want him feeling that I'm talking about him as if he wasn't there. I mean…" She stopped abruptly, working her lower lip the way she used to when a topic was too hard for her to put into words. Some things didn't change. He wasn't sure if he found comfort in that or not.

When she looked up at him, he realized that she'd bitten

down on her lower lip to keep from crying. Tears shimmered in her eyes. "I don't know where to start."

"Anyplace that feels comfortable," he told her gently, a well of old feelings springing forth. He smiled at her encouragingly. "Most people start at the beginning."

No place feels comfortable, Laurel thought. She was hanging on by a thread and that thread was getting thinner and thinner. Any second now, she was going to fall into the abyss.

Clenching her hands together, she forced herself to rally. She couldn't fall apart, she couldn't. She had to save Cody. Or, more accurately, she had to get Trent to save Cody, because if anyone could help her son, it was Trent.

SPECIAL MOMENTS™ 2-in-1

Coming next month

THE MILLIONAIRE'S CHRISTMAS WIFE by Susan Crosby

To seal a crucial deal, Gideon needed a wife. Denise Watson agreed to help – but what if their fake marriage could be for real?

A BABY IN THE BUNKHOUSE by Cathy Gillen Thacker

When Rafferty Evans offers a pregnant beauty shelter, the rancher doesn't expect to deliver her baby! Soon he finds himself opening his heart to love...and to an instant family.

THE HOLIDAY VISITOR by Tara Taylor Quinn

Craig McKellips stays at Marybeth's hotel every Christmas. But their slow-burning attraction is jeopardised when he reveals his identity...and his link to the past.

WORTH FIGHTING FOR by Molly O'Keefe

Jonah Closky has only come to the inn to meet his estranged family. He's distracted from his attempt to reconnect with them by gorgeous Daphne...a woman who he can believe in.

ALL SHE WANTS FOR CHRISTMAS by Stacy Connelly

She is determined to give Hopewell House's foster children the best holiday ever. And when a gorgeous businessman plays Santa, it might be Holly's happiest Christmas, too!

BE MY BABIES by Kathryn Shay

Lily Wakefield is pregnant – with twins! She should be off-limits to Simon, but the attraction is mutual. Then her past catches up and threatens to destroy everything...

On sale 20th November 2009

SPECIAL MOMENTS™

Single titles coming next month

THE CHRISTMAS COWBOY
by Judy Christenberry

Hank Ledbetter isn't the settling-down kind. Forced to give riding lessons to spoiled city girl Andrea, he's shocked to find himself hoping for a kiss underneath the mistletoe!

A STONE CREEK CHRISTMAS
by Linda Lael Miller

Vet Olivia O'Ballivan dreams of marriage and family, but her work consumes her. Until she is called to the ranch of guarded newcomer Tanner Quinn…

MISTLETOE AND MIRACLES
by Marie Ferrarella

Psychologist Trent Marlowe couldn't believe it when the woman he'd loved and lost asked him to help her little son. Must Trent put aside his past hurt in this season of forgiveness?

CHRISTMAS WITH DADDY
by CJ Carmichael

When unexpected fatherhood puts Detective Nick Gray to the test, Bridget Humphrey steps in as nanny. This carefree bachelor will have to become a family man!

On sale 20th November 2009

2 FREE BOOKS
AND A SURPRISE GIFT

We would like to take this opportunity to thank you for reading this Mills & Boon® book by offering you the chance to take TWO more specially selected books from the Special Moments™ series absolutely FREE! We're also making this offer to introduce you to the benefits of the Mills & Boon® Book Club™—

- **FREE home delivery**
- **FREE gifts and competitions**
- **FREE monthly Newsletter**
- **Exclusive Mills & Boon Book Club offers**
- **Books available before they're in the shops**

Accepting these FREE books and gift places you under no obligation to buy, you may cancel at any time, even after receiving your free books. Simply complete your details below and return the entire page to the address below. You don't even need a stamp!

YES Please send me 2 free Special Moments books and a surprise gift. I understand that unless you hear from me, I will receive 5 superb new stories every month, including a 2-in-1 book priced at £4.99 and three single books priced at £3.19 each, postage and packing free. I am under no obligation to purchase any books and may cancel my subscription at any time. The free books and gift will be mine to keep in any case.

Ms/Mrs/Miss/Mr _____ Initials _____

_____

Surname _____

Address _____

_____

_____ Postcode _____

Send this whole page to: Mills & Boon Book Club, Free Book Offer, FREEPOST NAT 10298, Richmond, TW9 1BR